W9-BXX-827

WITHDRAWN

CHOUETTE

Claire Oshetsky

An Imprint of HarperCollins*Publishers*

This is a work of fiction. Names, characters, places, and incidents are products of the author's imagination or are used fictitiously and are not to be construed as real. Any resemblance to actual events, locales, organizations, or persons, living or dead, is entirely coincidental.

CHOUETTE. Copyright © 2021 by Claire Oshetsky. All rights reserved. Printed in Italy. No part of this book may be used or reproduced in any manner whatsoever without written permission except in the case of brief quotations embodied in critical articles and reviews. For information, address HarperCollins Publishers, 195 Broadway, New York, NY 10007.

HarperCollins books may be purchased for educational, business, or sales promotional use. For information, please email the Special Markets Department at SPsales@harpercollins.com.

Ecco® and HarperCollins® are trademarks of HarperCollins Publishers.

FIRST EDITION

Designed by Angela Boutin
Part opener icons illustrated by Elizabeth Yaffe
Text break ornaments © Ekaterina/stock.adobe.com

Library of Congress Cataloging-in-Publication Data

Oshetsky, Claire, author.Chouette : a novel / Claire Oshetsky.
Description: First edition. | New York : Ecco, [2021] | Summary: "An exhilarating, provocative novel of motherhood in extremis"—Provided by publisher.
Identifiers: LCCN 2021003214 (print) | LCCN 2021003215 (ebook) |
ISBN 9780063066670 (hardcover) | ISBN 9780063066694 (ebook)
Classification: LCC PS3615.S39 C48 2021 (print) | LCC PS3615.S39 (ebook) |
DDC 813/.6—dc23

21 22 23 24 25   GV   10 9 8 7 6 5 4 3 2 1

To Patricia Taxxon

"Mother, they're still not sure it *is* a baby!"

—Mary X, *Eraserhead*

CHOUETTE

One

I dream I'm making tender love with an owl. The next morning I see talon marks across my chest that trace the path of my owl-lover's embrace. Two weeks later I learn that I'm pregnant.

You may wonder: How could such a thing come to pass between woman and owl?

I, too, am astounded, because my owl-lover was a woman.

As for you, owl-baby, let's lay out the facts. Your owlness is with you from the very beginning. It's there when a first cell becomes two, four, eight. It's there when you sleep too much, and crawl too late, and when you bite when you aren't supposed to bite, and shriek when you aren't supposed to shriek; and on the day that you are born—on the day when I first look down on your pinched-red, tiny-clawed, outraged little body lying naked and intubated in a box—I won't have the slightest idea about who you are, or what I will become.

But there you will be, and you will be of me.

We're in the kitchen in our Sacramento home when I tell my husband I'm pregnant. I don't even mean to say the words. My stew is simmering on the stove and its vapors tint the air the color of dog-skin and I can barely see the truth of things. My husband is leaning on the counter with a beer in hand, and he's been telling me about his day, in his usual upbeat tone, while punctuating his words with dazzling flashes of rational thinking.

"I'm pregnant," I say.

I'm afraid to look him in the eye. I look at the floor instead. I notice the floor could use a good mopping. I start to think about mops and the way they never get anything truly clean. Next I think about the way housekeeping is nothing more than a losing encounter with entropy. Did my husband hear what I said? Is it even true? Can I take it back?

And then my husband is hugging me, not gently but commandingly, and you could even say triumphantly. He is eleven inches taller and outweighs me by ninety-seven pounds. My feet come right up off the floor as he spins me around. When he sets me back down, I hear Arvo Pärt's plaintive duet for violin and piano, *Spiegel im Spiegel*, playing in my head, with all of its steady inevitability and sadness, and my life flows forward.

My husband says: "Hell. Wow. Oh. Hell. We've been waiting for this baby for so long!"

"Wait a minute," I say. "I have not been waiting for this

baby for so long. That is false. I'm not sure I want this baby at all."

My husband isn't listening. He spins me around some more until I get carried along by his mood, and the next thing I know the two of us are cavorting with joy in our somewhat grimy kitchen while we let the stew burn. Once the spinning is over and my feet are back on the ground, I'm left with a dizzying sense of loss. It happens like clockwork, they say. An owl-baby is born. This baby will never learn to speak, or love, or look after itself. It will never learn to read or toss a football. The father can see no single thing in this child that reminds him of himself. He thinks: "This isn't fair to me." And then he leaves. The mother stays.

"Come back, come back from wherever you are," my husband says.

I can tell time has passed because the dishes are dirty and my stomach is full and my husband is scooping the leftover stew into a plastic container. He is chattering away about becoming a father, a topic that leads him straight into telling me stories about his boyhood, and how his boyhood years shaped the man he is today. And then he tells me all about the future, and about what a good father he is going to be; and after that he swoops me up and carries me to our bedroom, where he makes love to me until I feel cherished and protected, and as precious as a glass figurine in need of constant dusting.

After our lovemaking my husband goes straight to sleep, leaving me alone and wide awake in the dark. I'm in mourning for my uncomplicated past, before I became pregnant with an owl-baby. I'm thinking about my music. I'm thinking about my owl-lover. I'm thinking about my life. I try to imagine adding an owl-baby to the mix. I'm a professional musician, a cellist, and I love my work. My pregnancy hasn't changed that yet. Maybe I can take the owl-baby along when I tour. Maybe I can give cello lessons while the owl-baby is gently napping. The owl-baby isn't buying it. My mind is flooded with broody owl-baby objections to my plans. It's trying to replace my selfish doubts with its own, yearning wonder about the life to come, outside the womb, if only I agree to be its mother. By morning I'm exhausted by the owl-baby's pleas. When my husband finally opens his eyes, I'm looking straight into them. All night long I've been waiting for him to wake up and take my side. All night long the whip-poor-wills and chuck-will's-widows have been screaming out their cold judgments of me from their tiny, brittle mouths, complaining about my lack of commitment so hatefully that I can't believe my husband slept through their rancor.

"Help me," I try to say, now that my husband's eyes are finally open.

But the owl-baby bites my tongue.

Just before my husband opened his eyes, I could still imagine that he had all the answers. Now that he is awake he looks stupefied. He yawns broadly and then he chews on his inner cheek. Soon his face breaks into a thousand smiles because he just remembered my delicate condition. He kisses me on the lips, eyelids, hair; and then he leaps up and volunteers to make us breakfast. He makes the coffee strong. He is doing his best to make me feel honored, and I do feel honored, like a sacrificial goat feels honored. Now we're munching toast together in the kitchen. My husband is an intellectual property lawyer in the patented-seed field, and he is already dressed for the job, in a starched-white shirt and trousers that he pressed himself. I'm still in my bathrobe. Our kitchen is one of those retro, rose-colored kitchens. The refrigerator is pink. The floor is black-and-white squares. The walls are the color of cleaned-up blood. The window looks out on a jaundice-yellow yard because I always forget to water the plants. The dishes from the night before are still in the sink. Soon there will be breakfast dishes to add to the pile. My kitchen and my world are spinning in all the wrong directions and I feel sick. My husband has just stopped reading the news on his phone because just now I got the words out past my lips that I've been wanting to say to him all morning, which are: "Help me."

There, it's done. I've said it.

The world rights itself.

He reaches across the table and grabs my hands.

"What is it?" he says. "What's on your mind? I love you. I'm here to help."

"You think this baby is going to be like you, but it's not like you at all," I say. "This baby is an owl-baby."

"Oh, honey, honey, honey," my husband says. "That's the jitters talking. Don't listen. I'm here for you. I love you."

Time passes and passes until finally we both cry a little.

"Maybe you're right. Maybe it's just the jitters," I say.

"Maybe it's just the hormones," he says. "We're in this together. I love you. You're having a feeling, that's all. We can talk more later."

He kisses the top of my head. He's already thinking about his workday. He kisses me again, this time on the lips, and then he goes out of the room briskly.

I hear a toilet flush.

I hear him whistling down the hall as if everything is settled.

I hear the front door open and close.

His car starts and I hear him drive away.

Now that my husband has left for the day, the owl-baby begins in earnest to attach itself and burrow in. I do my best to resist its insistent excavations. I'm determined to follow my usual routine. I teach three cello lessons in my home studio before noon. In the afternoon I work diligently on my transposition of Tom Johnson's *Failing: A Very Difficult Piece for String Bass*. I manage to focus so deeply on the work that I stop thinking about my pregnancy altogether, until my husband comes home an hour early, carrying a dozen roses. He observes aloud that I've neglected to make dinner, and then he says, in a jolly tone: "Never mind, honey, let's order takeout."

He phones in the order himself. Food arrives in tiny cartons.

We eat without talking.

After we're done, we pile the remains in the sink on top of

the dishes already there, and my husband suggests we play a few rounds of gin rummy.

And now he is deliberately losing, making clumsy mistakes.

He pretends to enjoy the game. He congratulates me after each play.

He's shuffling the cards for the next deal.

"It's an owl-baby," I say.

"Honey," my husband says. "Don't do this to yourself. Don't revisit the past. You're stronger than you know."

Lately my husband and I have fallen into the gentle habit of playing gin rummy together just after dinner. I love to watch him shuffle the cards. I love the way he can fit himself into the world so rightly. He's like a card in the deck that he has just squared up. I'm more like a card that somebody left out in the rain. I try to imagine that my husband's viewpoint may be completely right when it comes to this owl-baby. I try, at least, to nod my head and smile when he tells me how much he is going to love this baby, and what a good father he'll be. No good. I hear my own voice say: "You think it's a dog-baby, but you're mistaken."

"Don't indulge in those feelings, honey," he says. "It's not good for you. It's not good for the baby. It's been years since you've talked this way. You know it's all a fairy tale. Don't you?"

"This baby is an owl-baby. If I have this baby, it's going to kill me."

"Stop being so dramatic," my husband says. His voice is tight. He's getting impatient with me. "We're going to love this baby," he says. "I love this baby already."

"If I don't get rid of this baby, I'll die."

"Owl-baby! Dog-baby! Killer-baby! Baby-killer!" my husband shouts, and slams his fist down on the table.

Right away he apologizes.

"I'm sorry, I'm sorry," he says. "Oh, God, I'm sorry."

He gathers the cards together and begins to shuffle them in a performatively casual manner, and then he decides it would be best to apologize to me a few more times.

"I'm sorry. I really am. Oh, gosh. Of course, you're afraid. Of course, you're full of doubt. There's a new little person growing inside you. We've taken the leap. We've never been parents before and we don't know what to expect. Who wouldn't be afraid?"

"Listen to me," I say.

"Life can be scary sometimes. I get it. I do. I'm listening. I love you."

"It's a mistake. It's not even yours. Its other-mother is an owl."

My husband, who hates everything that he can't solve in an instant, and who just moments ago had been shuffling the cards on our kitchen table in a contemplative manner, hurls the entire deck of cards across the room. The cards thump on the wall and scatter explosively, landing on the counters, and the floor, and in the sink where the dishes are soaking in bilious water.

My husband walks away.

That's the end of the game.

After the card-throwing incident I avoid my husband for the rest of the night. I wait until he's completely asleep before I creep into bed next to him. As I lie here, listening to his gentle aspirations, I keep trying to inject myself with optimistic messages about the future. I try for hours, but it's hard to complete a single rational thought because the owl-baby is busy-busy interrupting each thought with chaotic and mysterious chitterings of its own, until the noise in my head grows so confused that I'm sure I'll never sleep again.

It turns out I'm wrong about not sleeping again, though, because the next thing I know I'm startled awake by a harsh daylight shining in from a little window near my bed.

My husband's side of the bed is empty.

It looks to be late morning.

Falling back to sleep is out of the question, and I decide to go out for a little walk. Outside, a bright sun beats and the air is filled with the cries of mourning doves. I walk along until I come across a woman who is painting daisies on her mailbox. The woman doesn't pay any attention to me. There is a little dog running about in the woman's yard, one of those high-strung, boisterous little dogs. It has a red rubber ball in its mouth. The dog and I lock eyes as I pass by. Almost as if an unspoken promise has been exchanged, the dog begins to follow me. To discourage the dog I cross to the other side of the street, but the dog still doggedly follows, trotting right along at my heel, stopping when I stop and speeding up when I speed up.

"Excuse me?" I call over to the woman painting daisies on her mailbox. "Can you call your dog, please?"

The daisy-painting woman doesn't look up. She's absorbed in her creative work.

Meanwhile the dog drops its little red ball between my feet and wags its tail.

Full of good intention, I pick up the grotesquely clammy ball and lob it gently in the direction of the dog's home. The dog skitters after it. I think I've solved my dog problem in a very clever way until a car comes around a corner and runs the dog right over. The dog doesn't even have time to complain about its fate before it's dead and gone. The car is one of those giant Cadillacs from bygone days and its springs are all shot and maybe that's why the driver doesn't notice such a small bump as this dog, because the driver keeps going. And the woman goes on painting. And I could go on walking. It's not really my fault. But I find myself crossing back over the street, where I stand, stupidly, until the woman notices me.

"What do you want?" the woman says.

"I'm sorry, but your dog has been hit by a car."

I try to say it gently. I gesture in the dead dog's direction.

The other woman's face fills up with rancid emotion, and her skin emits small sparks.

"That's not my dog," the woman says. "I hate that dog. That dog shits on my lawn all day. I don't even keep a dog.

Wait a minute. I don't even think that is a dog. That's just some crap in the road. What are you up to? Aren't you the one who keeps stealing aluminum cans from my recycling box? You are! You goddamn people!"

She jabs me in the chest.

"If I ever see you on my property again, I'll get my gun," she says. "Now git!"

Once I'm home from my walk, I throw on a jacket and find my keys and back my little car out and drive off. I don't have an appointment, but I like to think that the women where I'm going will be ready for someone like me to show up at their door. The building is low-slung and brick-faced, and the parking lot is full. I need to park across the street, and after that I need to walk past the people holding placards of aborted fetal remains enlarged to the size of four-year-olds. The maple trees that line the street are filled with crows. They're looking down on me, and judging me, but I'm immune to their shallow accusations. The waiting room is filled with pregnant teens holding hands with their best girlfriends. We respect one another's privacy by not looking one another in the eye. When a kindly-looking woman wearing a hand-crocheted cardigan calls my name, I follow her into a small cubicle and I tell her my story. I tell her everything. I tell her about my owl-lover—my dear, fierce tender-woman—and I tell her that the baby inside me is an owl-baby. I hate the sound of my voice because it's filled with a pathetic tremor. This woman passes no judgment over me. Her lack of judgment is so com-plete that she is useless to me. I'm irked that she won't take a stand. I long for her to take my hands in hers or to enfold me in a mother-hug and to say, "Of course you must get rid of it." She says nothing of the kind. Her detachment is a kind of torture. Tears spring from my eyes.

The kindly-looking woman in the cardigan hands me a box of tissues.

"No one can make this decision for you, hon," she says. "You take your time now, and cry all you like. Have a good little cry, dear. If you decide to go ahead, then let us know. Here is my card."

She puts her card on the table. She taps it twice. She steps out and closes the door so I can have my good little cry in privacy.

Now that we're alone together, the owl-baby gets busy-busy whispering in my ear, trying to convince me to give up. It tells me it's prepared to use force, but would prefer my full cooperation. I pray for a miscarriage.

As I'm driving back home from the clinic, I'm feeling so agitated and undisciplined that a painful memory from my childhood forces its way into my head—of the day when my father took me to the zoo.

We lived in a town that people used to call, with affection, a "sleepy one-horse town," until a rare ore was found in the hills and our "sleepy one-horse town" became a burgeoning city overnight. By the time I was born, there were piles of burning industrial waste encircling the perimeter of the city, and the air was turgid with smoke and soot, and the population had grown so large and so fast that the town had split into warring neighborhoods. My father told me that there were good neighborhoods, where the streets were straight and clean and well lit, and where the people doggedly followed the law; and there were bad neighborhoods, where streets were dirty and narrow, and crowded with hucksters and homeless degenerates, and where the people lived like wild animals. Between neighborhoods lay a border, where the gleaming met the gloaming. I lived with my parents quite close to the border, in a putty-colored house. If I looked out the front window, I could see a world that was ordered correctly along right angles, and if I looked out the back window, I could see wild eyes staring out at me from a shimmering, tangled thicket.

My mother suffered from chronic ornithosis, a disease of the skin that made her shy about going out and that left her bereft of friends and female companionship. I knew that she loved me, but I was never really sure if what I felt for her in return was love or just a brittle sort of pity. Her face was always hangdog, and I disliked the feeling of her corrugated diseased skin scraping against my soft skin when she held me.

My father, on the other hand, was gregarious and handsome. Every night he and his friends would gather around the hearth to smoke cigars and to share their bitter views about the world, until smoke curled into every corner of the house, and came wafting out from the cupboards when we opened them the next morning. My mother wasn't allowed to enter the room where these men gathered, unless it was to serve them food or to empty the ashtrays, but I was always made welcome. In those days I was a very pretty girl, and small for my age, almost like a tiny doll, and my father enjoyed dressing me up and making me do tricks for his friends. If his friends liked my tricks, then my father would reward me with little cakes. His friends would smile and bare their brown teeth, and pinch my cheek with their tobacco-yellowed fingers, so hard that I would bruise. Sometimes a man with big meaty shoulders might say to me: "I could just eat you right up, you pretty little thing! Wouldn't you like me to eat you right up?" And I would say: "Why, no, Mr. Meaty, I would like you to keep your hands off of me, please." My father would be ready to paddle me for my impertinence, but then he'd notice the way my brave, futile speech had made his friends all laugh, and he would feed me another little cake instead.

"Pretty little thing," the men would say.

"Pretty, yes, but stupid," my father would say brusquely, and then he'd send me from the room, and my mother, who had been listening from behind a door, would take me into her rough arms and tell me that she was proud of me, and that I shouldn't pay any mind to what my father said about me.

A day came along—the day that I'm remembering now—when my father took me to the zoo. The zoo in our town was poor and broken, and its prize animal, a giant Strix, was kept in a cage so small that the creature couldn't stand up properly. The creature kept looking at me through the bars, and it seemed to me that it was trying desperately to tell me something—that the two of us were the same, this Strix and I: that we were both sad, wild, perfect things.

"That's what you'll grow up to be, Tiny-girl, if you don't learn to obey me," my father said. "You'll be a wild thing that belongs in a cage. You behave like a wild animal already. You take after your mother."

The creature looked so sad to me. It licked its skin and so did I. It began to howl, and I, to scream. My father tried to pull me away, but I resisted. I scratched and bit. Soon the zookeeper came running. He had seen this kind of behavior before and came prepared, brandishing his paddle and swatting me several times before I fell silent and collapsed. My father carried me home and took me into a room without a lamp. "I'm going to fix you good," he said, and began to paddle me just as relentlessly as the zookeeper had paddled me. And although my mother was meek by nature, and typically did what she was told by my father, that night she flew to my side and defended me, so ferociously that my father fell to the ground, his mouth and eyes trapped in a permanent rictus of surprise. Then my mother snatched me up and fled with me straight into the gloaming, with only the blood-red moon to guide us. At first she was so agitated that she found the strength to carry me along in her arms as we ran, and when I grew too heavy for her to carry, she held me by the hand and pulled me along, so fast that my feet barely touched the ground; but as her excitement waned, and her stamina gave out, our pace grew slower and more labored. Soon her steps grew so slow and heavy that it felt to me as if my mother's feet must be sinking into the ground with each step. It took all my strength to pull her out again and to drag her forward. Her hand, dry and scaled from her chronic ornithosis, began to feel like a wooden claw.

"Ma, come on!" I whispered.

She let go of my hand.

"Ma?" I said.

My mother didn't answer. She gestured mutely toward her feet. Is it true that her long toes were burying themselves in the ground, so deeply that she could no longer take a step? Do I honestly remember seeing her two feet rooting themselves to the spot? Did her skin really become hard and rough all over, like a tree? Were there really spring-green leaves spilling forth from her fingertips? Or has my adult mind painted the memory of this night in such unlikely colors as a way to assuage my guilt for leaving her? I could hear men shouting and dogs barking, coming closer. Ahead I could see the tangled thicket. The wind in the trees sounded like the voices of women singing in chorus, and their voices were filled with glottal embellishments, as if sung by throats made of wood. The music urged me forward. And so I left my mother, and went on without her. I wasn't afraid because the trees took care of me, and brooded and bent over me, and sang to me their melancholy songs, and fed me, and gave me succor, until the Bird of the Wood found me and took me home with her and taught me to trust the sound of my own voice.

But now I can't understand why such a strange story should come flooding over my thoughts just as I'm driving home from the clinic in my little car. I'm so overcome by my own memories that I need to pull over and park, and I spend the next several minutes practicing my breathing exercises, while listening to the lovely cold relentless beauty of *Cantus Arcticus* by Rautavaara, a recording of which I always keep in my car, for times such as these.

Whenever my husband's extended family gathers together, they resemble a Northern European water polo team. At six foot three, my husband is the shortest of six brothers, and he is also the youngest. All of his other brothers have chosen wives of appropriate proportions. I'm the outlier. I'm known in the family as the tiny, fragile, photogenic little wife. My mother-in-law tends to seat me at the children's table for family gatherings. I don't think of it as a slight. It's more like an oversight. My mother-in-law sees right over me. She is six feet tall and never looks down. She looks out toward the horizon instead, with an expression on her face as if she is thinking the same thought all the time, and that her thought has something to do with pioneer spirit. She married a man who wears suspenders. She birthed and raised six sons on a generous parcel of land that used to be a fertile apple orchard, but is now a barren place of stunted, fruitless trees, sur-rounded by vast agricultural monocultures devoid of insect life. She still lives in the same house where she raised her six sons. After her sons left home, my mother-in-law channeled her mother-instincts into caring for exotic birds from rescue organizations, and dozens of these stricken creatures roam tragically about the grounds. Parrots. Toucans. Macaws. Peafowl.

You can tell these birds have led rough lives up to now. They are purblind and broken-winged. Their feet are missing. They hop pathetically about on mere stumps. They pick at the grit in the driveway as if to signal: Life is sad; life is sad. My mother-in-law doesn't care for these foster birds in the slightest—indeed, she frequently abuses them in small ways, by withholding food, and by forcing them to roam at night with no safe place to roost—but the birds give her home an exotic appeal that excites the women in her bridge club, and makes them feel jealous, and makes them wish they had exotic birds of their very own. My mother-in-law's grandchildren are forbidden to harass these pathetic creatures, but now and then one of the birds gets killed in the night by the dogs, and the grandchildren are permitted to bury it.

My father-in-law's suspenders are an affectation meant to give him the look of a country lawyer, and he is in fact a country lawyer, or was one, before he retired. He has begun to suffer from a mild semantic dementia, much to the embarrassment of his wife and sons, who want to think of this man as wise and rock-solid—the Atticus Finch of the West. Now that my father-in-law is retired, he has had the time to build a giant brick barbecue pit by hand. Just at this moment its expansive grill is covered in T-bones, because it's time for the Annual Summer Barbecue, and his entire clan has assembled. My in-laws live just eleven miles south of our Sacramento home, but whenever I arrive there, I feel as if I've traveled a migratory distance rivaling that of the arctic tern, to the edge of another world. The Central Valley sky that afternoon is so blue that it's white. Already the six sons are on the broad front lawn playing their vituperative game of volleyball. None of them has succeeded in life as magnificently as their father, economically speaking, and so they continue to compete for his affection, and to disguise their competitive animosity toward one another through sport, while their wives busy themselves in the kitchen making salads, and the children play together like a pack of dogs, and climb in the apple orchard, and chase my mother-in-law's rescue birds in spite of her rules, and jump and splash in the voluminous, extravagant family pool, where they hit one another over the head with pastel-colored plastic noodles. This swimming pool is part of the family lore. Each of the sons has pulled me aside at one time or another to tell his personal story of the time their father threw him into the deep end so he could learn to swim. Over the years, each of the six sons has told me his own personal near-drowning story proudly and with a reverential look on his face. Even my typically down-to-earth husband is transported by his own retelling of the time when it was his turn for his father to throw him into the pool. It's that kind of family.

It's time for me to be in the kitchen with the other wives, who are all busy with their little tasks, shredding cabbage and slicing beefsteak tomatoes into slabs and so on. Now and then the other wives try to engage me in conversation. But these other wives speak in concrete word-bricks, whereas I prefer to speak in metaphor: That way, no logic can trap me, and no rule can bind me, and no fact can limit me or decide for me what's possible. The downside of my communication approach is that it makes the yabber-yabber of everyday conversation a challenge for me, and so I tend to be quiet, mostly, at these family gatherings. My own little task that day is to cut grapes in half for the little ones. The little knife is sharp, and I keep thinking that the grape I'm about to cut is maybe my thumb. The wives have explained to me how it's necessary to cut grapes in half so that the little ones don't accidentally asphyxiate themselves by getting a whole grape stuck in their throats. I wonder why they protect their little ones so diligently from grapes only to leave them unsupervised in the family pool, supposedly to splash and play together while in reality they are busy forcing one another's heads underwater, and performing many other acts of one-upmanship that could well end in death.

As the wives toss and chop, they share stories about childbirth and menstrual woes.

The wifely conversations flow in and around me—

"My epidural didn't take, hell, I've never been in so much pain in my life—"

"No way, no way, no way will I ever go for vaginal birth next time—"

"They always warn you about the head coming through, but for me the worst part was the way her damn shoulder kept bang-bang-banging against my pubic bone—"

"My period comes every eight days and it comes out in big purple clots—"

"The potbelly never goes away—"

"I couldn't face another pregnancy, so I got a secret abortion and I still haven't told my husband—"

Just after this last bit of conversation, shared by the wife who is generally known in the family as the *secret aborter*, a random sweaty man barges into the kitchen. I'm flooded with alarm. I seize my little grape knife and hold it at the ready. But then realize it's not a random man at all. It's the *secret aborter*'s husband. He is incensed about the outcome of the volleyball game, and in search of lemonade. He breaks the mood. He doesn't care that the mood was different to begin with because he knows that nothing important ever happens unless he is there to witness it. He drinks, and then he rinses his glass, not really washing it, and goes out.

Today I have an important rehearsal with my string quartet partners. There's no time to waste because our concert season is nearly upon us. The violist has arrived before the rest of us. She's busy setting up our music stands in a clattering, unhappy way. I've always liked her because she is the kind of woman who strives at all times to be helpful and is never properly appreciated for her efforts, and in this way we're alike. I sit down and take my cello from its case. The colors in this room look subtly hostile. The noises in this room sound harsh and hollow. The bow in my hand feels like a hunter's bow. I search for my little sheath of arrows, but I can't find it anywhere.

The violist is scratching her skin.

"Does something smell rotten to you in here?" she says.

"I don't think so," I say.

"Really?" she says. "Something smells rotten to me. Like rotting meat. Like something died in the walls. You really don't smell it?"

I shrug and look away. I'm fairly certain that the violist is smelling me, but I'm hoping, through use of gentle misdirection, to get her to give up on trying to sniff me out. Now that I'm pregnant with an owl-baby, my scent is evolving into something rich and strange. Before this pregnancy I smelled like dollar pancakes on the griddle. Now I smell like molting feathers. The change is subtle, and in my opinion not unpleasant, and it's nothing like rotting meat, no matter what the violist says. No doubt she's suffering from some kind of olfactory hallucination. She often complains not only of peculiar smells but also of tinnitus and other ailments that only she can vouch for. She makes one pass around the room to locate the source of her discomfort, and then she gives up suddenly and settles into her chair. The first and second violinists come striding in. They are sisters from the Czech Republic, and they greet us in their charming Continental way, with kisses to each cheek, before they sit down and uncase their violins.

Today the four of us feel ready to run through our complete program without stopping. We begin with Mozart's "Dissonance" Quartet. The piece opens on a solemn, plaintively low C, rising up from the cello, a note that keeps repeating like a beating, broken heart, until suddenly the viola joins in—on a hallucinatory, high A-flat—and then the violins begin to play, each on a note so full of longing and surprise that it's all I can do to keep from dropping the bow. Suddenly an unwritten tritone comes clanging out from my strings. It's completely unexpected. It's a clumsy mistake. But we're professionals, and we press on. I can't find my equilibrium. I'm completely off balance. My fingers scrabble-scrabble over the fingerboard like wild animals. Echoes of memory and prophesy reverberate between my ears. I even hear myself begin to hum along tunelessly, as if I'm trying to remember an old song that I once knew by heart. I can't help it. The mistakes pile up. It's because of this owl-baby. It's telling me who is going to be in charge from now on. Is this what it means to be a mother, then? To be in constant, irrational conflict with one's own child? To be constantly challenged by the stubborn will of a creature who doesn't respond to logic or reason, and who always wins?

The first violinist is rapping her pencil on her music stand.

I stop playing.

Everybody does.

"So how did that go for everyone?" the first violinist says. "Thoughts?"

They all look at me.

"I'm sorry," I say.

"Let's try again from the beginning," she says gently.

We start over. We lurch forward. We try again. We try many times. My colleagues do their best to smooth over my chaotic wild scratchings with their soft clear harmonies, but it's no use. They keep telling me not to worry. We press on gamely.

It gets to be late afternoon.

"Well," the first violinist says.

"I think we've made very good progress here today," the violist says.

"I've played very badly," I say. "I've let you all down today."

"This is exactly what rehearsals are for," the violist says soothingly. "If we were perfect, then we wouldn't need rehearsals."

"We all have our days," the second violinist says. "I've had days of my own."

They're packing up their instruments as they smile and sigh and reassure. They tell me they believe in me. The violin-sisters both kiss me good-bye on each cheek. The violist rests her hand on my shoulder and smiles at me with warmth and understanding before she leaves. Now it's just me and the owl-baby, plus this cello between my legs, still warm from the kill. I'm not ready to go. I came to play music. I don't think the owl-baby likes Mozart, though, so I put it away. On a whim I bring out Anna Clyne's *Dance* and begin to play it. The music is new to me. The mistakes I make are my own.

"What do you think?" I say gruffly. "Do you like this music any better, you little scamp?"

I'm expecting the owl-baby to hijack my fingers at any moment, but it doesn't. I can feel it making soft, small somersaults inside. Maybe it likes this music. Maybe it's bored. Maybe it's happy. Who knows what an owl-baby thinks? The two of us are no longer at odds, at least. I play on. The owl-baby allows it. I play until I'm broken to pieces. I play until I've torn the bandage off. I play until I'm perfectly free.

Time is running out for me. If I don't make up my mind soon about this owl-baby, then I'll find myself accidentally careening into lifelong motherhood, but whenever I try to act in my own best interest, I hear a raucous soprano in my head, singing Schumann's "An meinem Herzen, an meiner Brust" with such wild, near-ecstatic abandon—*Only she who suckles knows what it means to be alive! I'm delirious with joy!*—that I can't think logically. I need to get away. I need my husband to come with me. I need him to take me to a quiet place and to hold me in his arms until these invasive and excessively optimistic thoughts about suckling leave my head, and then the two of us will come up with a plan, to save our lives.

"Honey, let's go away together for a few days," I say. "I need to. I need you."

My husband's teeth glint. Lately he's been nervous that I might run off to obtain a secret abortion, the way that, as almost everyone knows, a different wife in the family has secretly done.

"There is nothing I would rather do than take a small nip out of you," he says.

Or maybe what he says is: "There is nothing I would rather do than take a small trip with you."

But he's too busy at work to go away with me just now.

"Please," I say.

I say it in my very small voice, so small that my voice doesn't let on about the gravity of our situation.

"I need to work this weekend," he says casually. "And maybe next weekend, too. Maybe after that we can plan a weekend together. In the meantime, why don't you go stay with my mother for a few days? My mother will wait on you hand and foot, and then you'll come home right as rain."

He has failed me.

I buy a ticket from Sacramento to Berlin.

In Berlin no one can tell I'm American. I visit a museum full of Egyptian artifacts where I stand for a long time in front of the bust of Nefertiti. Nefertiti is encased in a plexiglass box, and she only has one eye, which gives her a nontraditional appeal. At first, I'm all alone with Nefertiti and the owl-baby, just the three of us in a silent, somber room, where the light is almost nonexistent—to preserve the artifacts— and the walls are painted Prussian blue. A pack of schoolchildren in uniform wanders in from the adjoining room. The schoolchildren are energized because they've just been to the room where the mummies are on display. The sound of their shrill happy voices electrifies the air. The owl-baby begins to flutter and caw inside me because it can sense that there are other young things nearby. I find myself meditating on the joy of children, and also on the life of Nefertiti, a mother whose divine lover came to her in the shape of a hawk. Nefertiti's lover, a day-bird, wore the sun as a crown. I wonder if the owl-baby, also the product of a mixed mating, will be anything like Nefertiti's god-children. I suspect that these thoughts are possibly not my own thoughts, but instead are the thoughts of the owl-baby, superimposed on mine. I wonder how long I've been the victim of subliminal messaging from a fetus. I wonder if it goes this way for all pregnant mothers: At first we fully recognize the existential threat that is growing inside us, but gradually evolutionary imperatives overcome the conscious mind's objection, and the will to reproduce overcomes the will to survive, and the needs of the baby overcome the needs of the host, until the only choice left for us women is to be willing, happy participants in our own destruction.

By this point in the trip I sound crazy even to myself. After spending so much time alone in Berlin—eating unexpectedly moist meals, visiting museums full of German schoolchildren dressed in aggressively militaristic uniforms, walking through a city so full of memory and artifact that there's a constant danger of falling into some year from the past and being lost there forever—it's hard for me to accept anything that I believe to be true about my life. Objectively it's all nonsense. The owl-lover. The owl-baby. The one-eyed bust of Nefertiti. The flight to Berlin. My music career. Berlin is where my music career first flourished, and so I'm not surprised that Berlin is where I've fled to contemplate my future life, whether that life will be as a famous cellist or as an obscure mother of an owl-baby. The last time I traveled to Berlin it was to give my debut performance of Dvořák's *Silent Woods* at the Berliner Philharmonie, and it was a triumph. "That such a tiny person can make such a majestic sound," one reviewer wrote. "Her playing is filled with otherworldly colors," wrote another. But there is always a danger, when traveling solo, that at some point everything about your life becomes ludicrous and unbelievable. You're alone most of the time, bombarded by your undiluted thoughts, and with nobody around to gently contradict you, your undiluted thoughts eventually spiral right out of control. Yes. That's what's happening to me. Undiluted thoughts spiraling right out of control.

I'm feeling so unsettled by my undiluted thoughts that I flee the museum by the nearest door. Fresh air will do me good. Once I'm outdoors, I find myself wandering through the Tiergarten, a part of the city that once was an old forest where deer and other game were hunted for sport by the nobility. It's dusk. Deer-shadows loom and leap in terror through the gathering dark. Before long I come to the Berliner Philharmonie, the famous concert hall designed in 1960 by the expressionist madman Hans Scharoun. I buy a ticket and go in. It's an all-Beethoven program. At intermission I visit the women's room, where I know there will be a long line, and if I join that line, I might feel like I belong in this world. But it turns out that I have nothing in common with the women in this line with me. All of them are in their nineties, or beyond their nineties. At any rate they are far beyond their reproductive years. I can't help but think of the way they must have spent their childhoods climbing through the rubble of broken buildings and running after US Army trucks in the fragile hope that a GI would throw them a potato or a candy bar.

After I reach the front of the line and do my business, I decide to leave the Berliner Philharmonie without hearing the second half of the program. To be honest I've heard enough Beethoven to last a lifetime. On the way back to the hotel I step into a German-looking eatery and order something from the menu called *Fleischbein* because it sounds festive. The waiter brings me the dismembered leg of a large animal, its broken femur sticking up from a clod of muscle. I attack it with vigor. There is a fish tank next to my table. The fish regard me anxiously, but I have no designs on them.

I've just put down my knife and fork so I can pick up the *Fleischbein* in my two hands and gnaw at the last scraps of meat with my teeth when I hear an owl shrieking outside. Since I'm in Berlin, where there are not so many owls, I know the shrieker must be my very own tender-woman, my beloved owl-lover, come to hash things out with me. Soon enough my owl-lover forces her way into this world, squeezing through the space under the door and spreading her monstrous wings wide. Owls have no sense of smell, and my owl-lover has no qualms about infusing the room with her rank odor, a unique mixture of feather and rotting rodent. Customers are so overcome by her presence that they rush out without paying. Cooks scoot out the backdoor emergency exit, so determined to get away that they neglect to turn off the gas burners. Soon the smell of caramelized food, and after that the smell of burning food, mix in with my lover's dead-rot smells. Smoke curls out from the kitchen. Alarms go off. Unlike the piercing, three-beat monotone of American alarms, these German alarms sound out in a richly rising, equal-pentatonic scale,

and I begin to wonder whether the difference in alarm har-
monics points to some fundamental difference between the
two cultures. Small fires are breaking out all over the room,
beginning with the paper serviettes. The fish are floating
belly up in their tank. Ceiling sprinklers begin to rain down.
My owl-lover and I gaze at each other with passion and regret.
I don't think I've ever been so sad. My lover's face is voluminous. I'm feeling the same mix of love and revulsion and
carnal attraction for her that I always have, and at the same
time I feel intensely unhappy to see her.

"My love," my owl-lover says. "I've come from the gloaming, to find you and to fight for you, and to bring you back
with me to the place where you belong. I love you. I've always
loved you. Come back. Come back with me, come be my only-
love again!"

"I'm pregnant," I say.

I note with cynical pleasure that she doesn't lift me off my
feet and spin me around many times, the way my husband did
when he heard the news. No.

"Pregnant," she says. "Well. What do you want to do
about it?"

I hear my own voice inside my head saying "Aha!" with
tremendous conviction because her reaction to my pregnancy
feels like a final confirmation of her callow, carnal nature.
She isn't one to make compromises for another, or to bend her
will to the needs of a child. Now I know I've made the right
choice to stick with my husband. My husband is kind, strong,
steady, normal, and a bit of a looker, whereas my owl-lover
is giant, musky, molting, monstrous, amoral, uncivilized, and

fickle, a creature I once loved and with whom I once or twice indulged in bestial acts. There really is no comparing them. The heat rises up from the small fires burning all around us until my heart grows as hard as a hard-boiled egg. I make myself forget the truth, that there was a time when my owl-lover was closest to my heart. There was a time when we clutched and scratched and cleaved. There was a time when we discovered such rapacious joys in each other that we would each bare our throats to the other, and cry out to be released. But I've changed, and she will never change, and now—as I look at her sitting across from me, pathetic and droopy, her face stained with soot and her feathers singed at the edges—I can't understand why I ever loved her.

"I'm in love with my husband," I say. "He takes care of me."

"He's broken you," my owl-lover says. "He's clipped your wings. He's a man. He's a dog. He'll never understand the monster underneath. Not the way I do."

"Don't talk that way about my husband," I say. "Life with you would be depraved and uncivilized."

Her round yellow eyes fill with tears.

"Won't you love me?" she says.

I close my heart.

"I've made my choice," I say.

"Then good-bye," she says.

She leaves by the window. She smashes right through. She has smashed right through my heart, too. The floor is littered with small pebbles of safety glass that sparkle in the fires. As soon as she's gone, I'm sure I've made a terrible mistake, and I rush out of there—but it's too late. She's already high in the air and flying away from me, one giant wing-beat following the next. I'm a creature of the ground and I can't follow.

I hear her sad laughter, trailing back, growing ever more distant.

I've made my choice.

Once I'm back in my room, I call my husband so I can remind myself how much I love him.

My husband picks up right away.

"I love you," I say. "I love you, I love you, I love you."

My husband informs me that our lawn has been invaded by pocket gophers and that the exterminator is coming that afternoon.

"I wanted to take care of the problem completely, before you came back," he says.

"Do you love me?" I say.

"Of course I love you," he says. "That's why I took care of it right away. I didn't want any leftover gas affecting our baby. The gas they use is deadly. That's the whole point."

I imagine the gas entering the burrows.

I imagine the mothers in the burrows, nursing babies with bare pink skin, and with eyes yet to open.

The day of my return flight comes around so fast that I still haven't made up my mind about the owl-baby. I've said good-bye to the owl-baby's other-mother, sure, but this owl-baby is still attached to me, and I to it, and whenever I try to listen to myself, and to sort out what I want—what I really want—all I can hear in my head is the sound an orchestra makes just before the concertmaster leaps onstage. It's a hushed nothing of a sound. My inner voice is silent. My owl-baby is silent. At cruising altitude the sea outside my window looks like wrinkled iron. Just as the sun begins to dip under the world's edge, the sea lights up like molten fire. After the sun sets completely, the sea looks like a swirling mass of viscous, poisonous silt.

Darkness falls upon the face of the deep.

I feel so alone. But I'm not alone. I feel the talons of my child grip me from inside. The grip is fierce.

Love me, the owl-baby pleads.

I look out into the void.

I see my own face reflected back.

It dawns on me that I'm blaming this blameless baby, all because of an argument with its other-mother.

I think: It doesn't seem so bad a fate, does it? To love this child?

And then I think: I'm going to be a mother, after all.

As soon as I'm done thinking this last thought, the sun begins to rise on the opposite horizon and a flash of gold ignites the earth back to life; and it seems as if this sunrise, so beautiful and golden, has been choreographed just for me, to encourage my surrender. The world below begins to order itself into recognizable patterns of green and gray, and the plane touches down, and before I know it, I'm breathing the stale air of the airport terminal and my husband is hugging me like I've returned from the dead.

My husband's childhood was the color of fresh laundry, and the voice of his childhood was the voice of his mother calling him to supper. My childhood was the color of blood, and the voice of my childhood was the voice of wild crepuscular things rejoicing in the dusk. My husband remembers his childhood as perfect. I remember my childhood as less than perfect. No wonder my husband and I don't always see eye to eye.

But at this moment, as I'm standing in this stale airport with my husband, we *do* see eye to eye: My husband is looking straight in my eye, and I'm looking straight in his eye, and we're hugging each other, and I can tell that we're going to have this goddamn baby together no matter what. We're sharing this truth so fiercely that his kisses feel like small bites and the air is full of gun smoke. I say to him, "We're going to have this goddamn baby, aren't we?" and he says to me, "Yes, yes, we're going to have this goddamn baby, and it's going to be the luckiest goddamn baby in the world, because this baby is going to have me for a father, and you for a mother." We hug some more, and he cries in a manly way where the tears remain in his eyes and don't actually fall anywhere, and then we collect my case from the baggage claim area. On the way to the car we're so full of wonder that we don't say a word. My ears are ringing. My skin is numb.

Just as we merge onto the highway, my husband opens all the windows in the car. Now we're traveling along with the wind roaring in our ears. Air rushes in and out of our bodies as if our lungs were bellows. Dead dry leaves fly in through the windows and rattle against our skin before flying out again. I wonder whether all this commotion on my husband's part is because he hasn't come to terms with the way I smell these days. I no longer smell like dollar pancakes. I'm going to be a mother now. My body forevermore will be rich with musty, maternal emanations. It's what he says he wants. Didn't he know that a fecund gamey smell is part of the bargain when a woman becomes the mother of an owl-baby?

Once we get home, he opens all the windows in the house.

"I think you need a good bath," he says, and laughs to take the sting away.

"That's not what I need," I say.

To honor my husband, though, I draw a hot bath and scrub and scrub my skin and my hair. The water turns green, and then gray. I let the water drain out and draw another bath. I know it's pointless. I'm going to be a mother. I've accepted it. My body is riparian. I'm filled with growing things.

Two

As soon as I get out of my bath, I telephone the first violinist to tell her that I'm back from my trip to Berlin.

"You were in Berlin?" she says.

And after the briefest pause—the most delicate caesura imaginable—she adds: "How was the trip?"

I'm so relieved. I was worried she might be unhappy with me for flying off without telling her and the others. It's true, I've missed a few rehearsals, and we do have our concert season coming up, but she seems to understand. Our conversation has fallen straight into a lovely harmony. I'm thinking things are going quite well between us when she interrupts me to say: "Well, Tiny, truth be told, after we didn't hear from you for many days, we began to rehearse with another cellist."

I don't say anything. Because I'm stunned.

"We had no choice," the first violinist says. "The concert season is nearly upon us. You know how it is."

"I'm pregnant with an owl-baby," I say.

I say it because I want her to feel sorry for me, and to welcome me back the way I deserve to be welcomed, but my strategy backfires. Her jangle-thoughts are so loud that I can hear them coming straight through the telephone wires. She's noisily thinking that, with an owl-baby on the way, my mind will be muddled, and my playing will be punctuated by chaotic rumblings, and I'll never come up to speed before the concert season comes along. But she's too kind to say any of that. Instead she calmly tells me: "I'm so happy for your news, Tiny. If you mean it when you say that we can count on you from now on, and if you promise to work as hard as you can to regain our trust, then I'll call our new cellist. I'll tell her that we'll be rehearsing with you this afternoon. That's all I can promise. Come this afternoon. After that, we'll see."

Her voice is filled with probationary timbres.

"I'll be there," I say.

When I get there, I can tell right away that the first violinist has informed the others of my gravid condition. All three of them keep casting glances at my lower abdomen and making disapproving, smacking sounds with their lips. They're thinking, "How can she commit to the work, with an owl-baby on the way?" and "Won't an owl-baby put the kibosh on our spring tour?" and "Do we need to hire a lawyer to get us out of her contract?" We begin with the Mozart, of course, since it didn't go so well the last time we rehearsed it. I can tell that they're all bracing themselves for some exotic, nonconforming note to sound out from my instrument. They don't need to worry, though, because we haven't even played past the first dozen notes in the score before the owl-baby swims into my fingers and makes them swell up.

I can't press my fingers to the fingerboard.

The slightest pressure brings on blood blisters.

I can't hold the bow.

It's the owl-baby's fault.

"Oh, that doesn't look good at all," the violist says.

"Looks serious," the first violinist says. "You should rest those hands. Go home, Tiny, and rest those hands. We'll carry on somehow without you."

The second violinist is studying her music with pursed lips.

"Give me a moment," I say. "It's some kind of reaction. It will settle down."

The first violinist is looking at her phone. No doubt she's looking up the number of the replacement cellist.

The second violinist is studying the music.

The violist's skin is flushed with pity.

I put my cello back in its case and snap it closed.

"I guess I'll go home and rest these hands," I say.

"Take care," the second violinist says.

"Maybe it's for the best," the first violinist says.

The violist emits a mournful sigh to show that she's on my side.

"Good-bye for now," she says.

As soon as I shuffle out, the three of them begin to play something new together. They have put the quartet music away. Now they're boisterously attacking a piece that doesn't need the cello: Dvořák's famous *Miniatures* for viola and two violins. The music bullies me down the long hallway and pushes me out into the world.

I'm back in my little car, driving home.

Never mind, never mind, the owl-baby says. *I'm all you'll ever need.*

That night I wake up with a start when the owl-baby unmoors itself from the womb and begins swimming inside me with muscular agility. The owl-baby is in its early Cambrian period, but it's far enough along to be classified as Chordata. Its flippers are powerful. It's still more fish than bird. It begins to explore the world inside me with bacchanalian abandon. When the owl-baby swims behind my eye and commands me to open it, I discover that we can see in the dark. Instead of the black void, I see photons spinning out in all directions, and the owl-baby cries in delight, and so do I.

"Cluck, caw caw caw!" we rasp.

"What is it, what is it?" my husband says fitfully in his sleep as he rolls onto his back. Why does sleep lie so close to death? My husband's skin is waxen. I feel a sudden terror that I'm going to lose my husband somehow—and if I did, what would become of *me*?—and I kiss him many times on the lips until he opens his eyes and smiles.

"What is it?"

"I felt the baby move."

He forgets all about my musty emanations and pulls me into his arms, and then he rests a warm flat hand on my belly, and when he feels a fishlike movement under his fingers, he begins to cry freely. I hold him. We cry together, but for different reasons.

By morning the owl-baby's sense of the world has grown so refined that it can sense the frozen chicken livers trying to hide inside the freezer. It reacts with such intense pleasure that it forces me to open the freezer door and to get the livers out. As we tear into the livers, the owl-baby lifts its head inside me, and flutters its new bits of wings, as if to say: "Eat, pretty mother, and build your nest for me!" The livers melt and congeal in my mouth. I swallow and feel the livers slide down my gullet. There's no turning back. I'm as bound to this baby as I am to my own beating heart.

Later in the day I dig up grubs in the garden and watch them convulse in my palm. I let the telephone ring.

By afternoon the owl-baby has persuaded me to contact my cello students one by one and to cancel their lessons. Next I call my string quartet partners—first the second violinist, then the violist, and finally the first violinist—to let them know I won't be coming back for a while. I give them my blessing to call in a temporary cellist for the time being.

"Oh, I'm very sorry to hear that," they say.

The owl-baby objects to the word *temporary*.

Once my phone calls are done, the owl-baby amuses itself by rummaging through my digestive tract.

The days and hours keep coming on until it's time for my sonogram. The doctor gels me up, and then she moves the monitor so that my husband and I can get a good view of the owl-fetus. The doctor touches her sonic wand onto my greased-up belly. My husband is overcome by a complex emotion. He squeezes my hand painfully. I see the owl-baby inside me for the first time. It opens its beak and covers its ears with its tiny, cramped claws.

"Perfectly normal," the doctor says.

"I don't think the owl-baby likes the sound of the sonogram," I say.

Your tiny claws are pressed against the sides of your head and your little mouth is open.

"Stop what you're doing," I say. "You're hurting it."

"Studies show that a sonogram causes no lasting damage," the doctor says. "You're interpreting a perfectly normal fetal gesture as pain."

She rolls her sonic wand some more, deep into the belly grease.

Your talons are cramping inward.

Your beak is open and screeching.

"You're hurting the owl-baby!" I shout. "Stop it!"

The doctor withdraws her sonic wand.

She looks at me with eyes as soft and indulgent as the eyes of a basset hound.

"What the hell are you talking about?" my husband says. "Owl-baby! I thought you were over that! My wife does this to herself, Doctor. She gives in to hysterical fears. She thinks our baby is going to be deformed or retarded."

"These days we prefer to use terms like *disabled* and *developmentally delayed*," the doctor says, and then she turns to me.

"Little mother, we've done all of the recommended prenatal tests," she says. "Your fears are perfectly normal and you have nothing to fear."

"Your so-called recommended prenatal tests are wrong over half the time," I say. "I read about it in a magazine. Also, you're testing for the wrong things. You haven't given me a single owl-baby test."

I think I've eviscerated her argument, but she drones on as if I've said nothing at all.

"Pregnancy is a very special time in every woman's life," she says. "It's natural to be fearful. We're almost done. Just a few more seconds. It's important for your child's health that we finish the job."

She touches her sonic wand to my greased-up belly with conviction. She points out the salient features of what she considers to be your perfectly normal self. Soon I lose track of her yabber-yabber, owl-baby, because I'm watching you on the monitor. I'm watching the way you have taken a piece of my uterine wall into your beak. I'm watching the way you're shaking your head back and forth ferociously, with a piece of me in your beak, as if you're in so much pain that you're ready to rip your way out of there.

"My God, that's beautiful," my husband says. His voice is choked with feeling. He kisses me many times.

That night I wake up with the moon in my eyes. I may as well face it: I may never sleep through the night again.

As usual my husband is sleeping soundly on his back next to me. By moonlight his skin is silver, and his dreaming face is full of raptures. He looks as young as he did when I was lost and he first found me. My husband has kept up his old habit of thinking I'm a woman in constant need of his protection and advice. I don't resent it. I'm in love with the habit of his steady love. I want to wake him and tell him how much I love him, and why; but his face is very sweet, and so I leave him to his dream-rapture, and get up and go to the kitchen, where I make myself a cup of "twig tea," which I've been told has special properties to help reluctant mothers accept their fates.

To celebrate the next inevitable passing of the season, my husband's pale Nordic family gathers together for their annual Thanksgiving Feast. The day is Central Valley fair. The air is so warm that my husband and his brothers have pulled off their T-shirts to play their biannual vituperative game of volleyball. The children splash in the pool with nearly as much zest as they did in July, at the Annual Summer Barbecue. Once more I find myself in the kitchen with the wives. My tiny important job of the day is to crimp pie crusts. As I crimp, the wives take turns caressing my protruding bulge. I feel herniated. I feel as if my insides are about to pop out my navel. I'm not interested in the taste of food. At midday we come together like a pack of dogs to feed upon the slaughtered bird. My mother-in-law keeps staring across the tables in my direction. I can tell that she's scheming to get me alone at some point so that she can impart her mother-wisdom to her pregnant daughter-in-law. All of her children are perfect dog-children, and her grandchildren, too, so I doubt that her mother-wisdom will count for much. Later that evening, when the wives have finished washing the dishes and are busy putting their children to bed, and when my husband and his brothers are drinking beers on the pool deck, their laughter rising like barks that echo in the trees, and after my father-in-law has gone to bed following an embarrassing attack of semantic dementia, it's just the two of us, my mother-in-law and me, standing together antagonistically on the front porch at dusk. We're looking out over the world as evening passes into night. We're two people in a pastoral scene. I'm the short pregnant one in the scene.

"You don't even know my grandchildren's names, do you?" she says suddenly. "Before my son married you, I said to him, 'Son, if you want children, then you better find somebody else to marry, because this one is *not interested* and *not qualified*. She is *not like us*.' As I've been saying to my son for years—"

I gaze out over the purple-dusk lawn while my mother-in-law continues with her yabber-yabber. Before long my mind begins to wander. My mother-in-law's voice never arrives at a natural stopping place. It's a way of speaking that encourages woolgathering in me.

"Can you honestly say to me, right now, that you have a single *mother-bone* in your body?"

I have fallen into a standing doze.

"You don't really belong in this family, do you? You don't really belong anywhere in the real world, do you?" my mother-in-law says. "Hey now! I'm asking you a question!"

"Are you?" I say.

"Don't be vague," she says. "Isn't that just like you, to be vague. Here I am doing my best to give you practical advice. You don't have the *mother-bone*. You need my guidance. You need to get your feet on the ground. No more histrionic gestures. No more breakdowns. No more flights of fancy. You're going to be responsible for a small and precious life. You can't be indulging yourself in one of your moods while your child is walking into traffic or setting himself on fire."

I can't quite follow her logic because I've become distracted by her flock of rescue birds on the lawn—the partridges with buckshot in their bodies, and the peacocks with missing feet, and the debeaked cockatoos whose freakishly long life spans never fail to outlast the human need for cockatoos, and the many other sorry birds that my mother-in-law has given refuge to over the years. In the last few minutes, as my mother-in-law droned on, these birds have made their slow way toward us, across the broad lawn. Their movements are halting but purposeful. I'm a little bit in awe of them. They look like a solemn procession of wounded veterans, full of dignity in spite of their war wounds. My awe increases when other, wilder birds—starlings and pigeons, and geese, and crows, even an escaped parrot or two—funnel down from the dusk and fill the air all around with their calls and their wing-beats.

Over by the pool deck my husband and his beer-drinking brothers have set down their beers and have stood up from their lawn chairs. All six brothers are standing in exactly the same posture, with clenched fists at their sides. They're looking skyward. Their faces harden into defiant lines as their hackles rise. They sense a danger to their kind. They wish they had their guns.

By this time many dozens of birds are swirling in the air like ticker tape while the rescue birds whoop and sing and stump forward on their broken stumps. Their song is dissonant, but somehow familiar. Before long, this cacophony of voices finds its natural order, and I realize to my wonder that the birds are singing a passable a cappella rendition of *Oiseaux Exotiques*, by Olivier Messiaen—a modern lawless musical composition if there ever was one. And then the birds swerve away from Messiaen, and the dissonance resolves into a new song, sad and serene, and full of harmonic resonance, and even though the little throats of these birds are unaccustomed to forming human speech, I can make out their words quite distinctly: *"Ave mater, gravida noctua!"* they chant, over and over again, as if they are seeking my solemn vow to be a good mother to this owl-baby. All the while my owl-baby punches and tumbles inside me until I need to grab onto the porch railing to keep from falling over. And in that moment, grabbing on for dear life to that porch railing while surrounded by this bright bold gaggle of birds, I'm overcome with the beauty of the wild world, and I weep a little, to think that the owl-baby chose me and not some other mother who might not have had the stamina to care for such an exceptional young life. I begin to understand what a gift I've been given, to have been chosen for this task. The truth overwhelms me, and humbles me. The birds are telling me that my life's work, as your mother, will be to teach you how to be yourself—and to honor however much of the wild world you have in you, owl-baby—rather than mold you to be what I want you to be, or what your father wants you to be. And as this bird-miracle unfolds around us, so beautiful and mysterious, my mother-in-law remains deeply trapped inside her earnest, plodding lecture, until I begin to laugh, because my mother-in-law surely knows the facts about all things and yet she doesn't notice the truth all around her. The owl-baby laughs, too, and before long the two of us grow so raucous and disrespect-ful that my mother-in-law wakes up from her Polonius-like stupor, and then she does notice the birds, and she screams and shouts and scuttles crabwise from the porch, chasing after them with maniacal, violent purpose, yelling "Git, git!" in her smoker's baritone, while flailing her arms.

The spell of birds is broken.

Birds skitter off into the night, with the exception of my mother-in-law's rescue birds, and they stump back quietly to their characteristic pathetic huddle on the patch of lawn growing over the septic tank.

My mother-in-law staggers back onto the porch, looking winded and terrified.

"Those dumb beggars," she says. "Those birdbrains. Always looking for a handout. Birds never show affection unless there is food in your pocket. I swear they'd eat me alive if I didn't feed them. I don't know why I bother."

We close that year's Thanksgiving Feast in the same way we do each year, with the ceremonial dollar-pancake break-fast in the morning. The only deviation from past tradition is that my father-in-law stays in bed that morning, rather than joining us, because his semantic dementia has become too painful for the rest of the family to witness, and they have all agreed to sequester him for the sake of the grandchildren. The eldest son, who makes his living as a chiropodist, takes his father's place at the head of the table. No one mentions the absent patriarch. After we finish eating our meal of dollar pancakes, the wives perform the ritual of making leftover-turkey sandwiches and wrapping them up in wax paper for everyone to take home with them. My husband and I drive home with our turkey sandwiches. We eat them for dinner that night. The days pass. The owl-baby growls and grows inside me until a night comes when I'm lying in bed next to my slumbering husband—who has taken to quietly wearing an air filter at night, on account of my gamey odor—and a stark interrogative light shines through a window near my bed, waking me. The owl-baby wants to go for a walk, so off we go. Outside the air is filled with early-morning damp, and my soul feels weighted down by the mistakes of my past. Small creatures chitter in the leaves of giant oaks lining the street. It's autumn, and the oak leaves are richly red. Before long I come to the woman painting daisies on her mailbox, and what's more, here is the same dog, alive and well and not run over by a big Cadillac, and with the same slavered red ball in its mouth. Is it so easy, then, to recover from our mistakes? To have a do-over? The idea heartens me. The little dog is alive. It's as if my choices from the past have been erased and I can begin with a clean slate. I gently touch the daisy-woman's shoulder, to catch her attention. Now that the dog is alive, I want to ask her if she recognizes it. Maybe I can help the dog find its true home.

"Excuse me, do you know who this dog belongs to?" I say.

The woman leaps up.

Her eyes grow round and globular.

"As a dog returns to his vomit, so a fool returns to his folly!" she roars, and shoves me into the street, just as a big Cadillac turns a corner and runs me down like a dog.

The next thing I know I'm wrestling with a damp sheet in the dark in my own bed with my husband's heavy hot arm draped over my hips. I can feel the gritty asphalt ground into my skin. I can smell my own blood. I can hear the soft patters of the wild things, scratching at the windows, trying to get inside. I'm holding on to my husband's arm so tightly that he wakes up, shouting: "What is it! What is it?"

"There's been an accident. I'm bleeding."

"You're bleeding!"

He wakes up entirely and turns on the bedside lamp and flings back the sheets and pulls my legs apart and looks between them.

"No, no, it's all right!" he shouts. "You're not bleeding!"

He sighs his masculine sigh and then he performs a pantomime of looking my whole body over, patting me gently here and there, as if I'm a child in need of reassurance following a nightmare instead of a grown woman who has just been run down in the street like a dog, and who is also, let's not forget, pregnant with an owl-baby; and when my husband is done with his cursory look-over, he kisses my belly with a definitive smack.

"Nothing," he says. "Just a dream."

Ever since I've come home from Berlin, my husband has tried his surreptitious best to avoid being near me unless there is an open window close by. He's not alone in his struggle to be near me. Strangers give me wide berth in restaurants. The casual web of relationships I've built up over the years that I've lived in this neighborhood with my husband—ties that bind me to this community, just because I'm human and alive—erode within weeks of my owl-baby commitment. The mail carrier hurries along instead of greeting me the way she has for years. The grocery store clerk who knows me by name closes up her line when she sees me coming. The homeless person waiting outside the grocery store covers her nose with her raggedy sleeve and pushes her shopping cart rapidly away instead of waiting for the dollar I hold out.

"What's wrong?" I say to my husband, even though I know what's wrong. "Why don't you want to be near me any longer?"

"Nothing's wrong," he says.

"If there's nothing wrong, then come sit here next to me on the sofa. Let's watch TV together."

He sits next to me on our little sofa just to prove I'm making it up.

Soon he finds an excuse to leave my side.

A few days later my husband begins to sleep in the little apartment above our detached garage. At first he says that it's just for a night, and then it's for a few nights a week, and then it's where he sleeps all the time. He may love me, but he doesn't want to smell me. I begin to understand the nature of my sacrifice. I'm pregnant with an owl-baby. Everyone is a little bit repelled by me. Everyone is a little bit uncomfortable. Everyone can tell that I'm about to enter a world where women sit alone in the silent corners of cafeterias, spoon-feeding their grown children, while others look away.

A morning comes along when, just after my husband leaves for work, I hear a very tiny voice, the tiniest voice ever, speaking to me from a place I can't locate. It's such a tiny voice that, in the beginning, I'm not even sure if the tiny voice exists, or if it's speaking in words, or if it's just yabber-yabber from somebody's radio next door.

I try to locate the voice.

Eventually I realize the voice is coming from inside me.

It's almost as if I can hear the owl-baby-voice inside me, asking me a question.

Can you fly? the little owl-baby-voice says from inside me.

Or maybe: *Can you die?*

Or: *Can I?*

Or: *Why?*

And all of these questions seem to me to be very good, very precocious questions; only I can't be sure of which question it is, or even if these questions are made up of actual words or are instead made up in my own head. All I know is that the voice is very tiny and very dear to me.

"Is that you, owl-baby?" I say.

I shout to be heard, as I'm not certain just how sound travels through the body to the ears of a gestating fetus.

"I'm here! What do you want?"

I listen. I'm a little scared of what I might learn next. But I'm your mother now, and it's my job to understand you. I make up my mind to listen with all my heart. I empty my mind of all doubt. I yield to you.

At first nothing happens.

But then a sudden, carnal, electric force—akin to religious rapture—flows through me, and every cramp and worry, whether lodged in my limbs or in my thoughts, is released and flies away; and all that is left in me is the need to escape—to get out of this four-cornered box—because the right-angled ugliness of the indoors is terrifying to me.

We climb straight out the window, you and I. I'm shot like an arrow from a bow. We are running, flying down the street together. Bare feet; bare heads; bare mouths open and in search of the taste of blood. Our predatory joy is so strong that we can feel the dream of wings. We can see our feathers unfurl. Our eyes lock forward. I imagine my neighbors on either side, peering casually out their windows to see if the morning paper has come, only to see a wild, predatory woman flash by, a woman who is so overcome with mother-love that she is leaping and flying down the street. My neighbors say to themselves: "Hey, isn't that the woman from the next block? Has she finally lost her mind completely?" They would do well to withhold judgment, though, and to expend their energy instead with bringing their children and their small pets inside, for safety's sake. I close our eyes until they are half lidded against the harsh bright day, and we turn our gaze inward, owl-baby, you and I, toward the needs of our beating hearts; and our hearts tell us where to run, to an open field full of foxtails and the rusted carcasses of automobiles. We hide in the thicket. We crouch and wait.

We sense small creatures all around us, holding their breath, hoping we pass by.

Britten's "Bordone" is playing softly and resonantly between my eyes until the music's patient drone turns me to stone.

I am fossilized.

A rustle in the grass.

Our talons curl forward, and we strike.

I open my eyes in the dark. I close my eyes. My head hurts. My jaws pulse. The taste of iron tacks fills my mouth and my feet are nettle-stung. I hear my husband's car pull into the driveway and the engine stops, and I hear him get out and slam the door, but I don't hear his familiar jaunty step along our concrete walk toward the front door.

"Christ! What the hell!" my husband shouts, as if from a far distance.

I hear his footsteps trudge in an unexpected detour, along the side of the house. I feel content and well-fed, and curiously interested in the movements of my spouse, but not enough to move from my spot. I open my eyes in time to see the shadow of his form pass slantingly across the window. I hear the toolshed door creak open and shut. I hear the steps trudge back again. I hear the scrape of shovel on concrete, and then I hear the sound of a trash lid slamming shut; and then the squeak of the hose bib, and the sound of water rushing through the hose; and then small splashes, landing on the front walk, just outside the door.

Then nothing.

The door opens.

He flips the light switch on.

"What were you doing sitting in the dark?" my husband says.

It didn't feel dark to me. I see everything. I close my eyes against the tiresome glare.

"There was a goddamn dead possum lying on our front walk," my husband says bitterly. "Huge. Gutted. Half eaten. What a mess. A big one. I cleaned it up. God, the smell."

"Thanks," I say.

"But seriously," he says. "Just gutted."

"Mmm."

"So, what were you up to, sitting here in the dark?"

"I don't know," I say. "I must have dozed off."

My husband nods and sets down his briefcase. He hangs up his suit jacket in the front closet, and after he's done, he just stands over there, over by the door, looking at me curiously. Not coming closer. Just looking me over.

"There's some grass in your hair," he says.

The world outside my door slides into midwinter in the bland manner of a place without remarkable seasons. My husband tells me that he needs to fly to Sydney urgently for a trade conference. His warm large hand is holding my cold tiny hand. My due date is still well over a month away, but he's feeling worried and solicitous, and he asks me over and over again if he should stay home rather than going to his important trade conference in Sydney. He wants me to say, "No, of course you should go to your conference," and that's what I say. He puts his arms around me gratefully and I snuggle in. My husband has been touching me less and less, not just because he's revolted by my gamey scent, but also because he's disoriented by my enormously pregnant shape. It's as if a bowling ball has come between us. He's not sure how to grab hold of me any longer. His stony strong arms enclose me and I realize how much I've missed him. When I feel his breath on my hair, it's as if I've returned to a beloved country. In spite of my best intentions, though, even as I rest in my husband's arms, I can't help but think back on the feathery flatness of my owl-lover's embrace, and to compare my two great loves.

My owl-lover had a manly lack of mammaries, but otherwise she was all woman. I used to love the way she could flex her feathers separately, moving her feathers across my skin like a thousand soft feather-fingers. My husband's chest is also nice, though, especially because he's here with me, right now, in a world of dependable right angles, whereas my owl-lover is far away in the gloaming, living in a wild thicket and hunting small rodents for her dinner. I listen to my husband's living heartbeat in my ear, drowning out the memory of my owl-lover's lighter, faster heartbeat. I tell myself again what a good decision I've made to raise up this owl-baby with the help of a slow-and-steady-heartbeat kind of partner like my husband, and not with a rapid-flight-fluttering-heartbeat kind of partner like my owl-lover. I'm trying to feel as much as my small body could ever feel while my husband holds me so that I can remember later how much I really loved my husband on the day he left for Sydney, but my body seems to know, even as my husband is holding me, that we will never again be as close as we are now, right now, in this embrace, at the time when I'm eight months pregnant with an owl-baby, and my husband is about to fly away from me.

A late-winter day comes along when the air is clean and unusually brisk. My husband is still in Sydney at a trade conference and I don't blame him for that. There is snow-dust on the ground. The light coming through my window is full of uneasy expectation. I grow concerned that an unscheduled eclipse is about to take place. My due date is a month away, but even so I break out into an anxious sweat. To calm myself I decide to take a cool shower. The water hits my skin like bits of cinder. My naked wet belly is huge and distended. As I soap my belly, a sudden thing bulges out: a heel or an elbow. The movement is so revolting that I need to flee my body for several hours. When I return to my body, I'm in labor. To avoid any fuss, I call 9–1–1 and the people come. They are calm, except for the driver, who engages the siren and takes the corners so fast that the gurney they have strapped me on jolts hard to the left, and hard to the right, and the leather straps dig into my ribs. My nails have grown thick, and there is blood under them and bits of skin. I bite my tongue and drip fresh scarlet down the sides of my mouth. I want to peck out the guts of the one who leans over me, and to suck out the soft parts, but before I can, the ambulance stops with a shudder and the back doors fly open. I pass over the event horizon.

"Get her feet in the stirrups!" a voice shouts.

Above the surgical mask my doctor's eyes are the color of canola oil.

His eyebrows are the color of sour cream.

On the next push something crowns and then the head is out and the rest slips through.

Doctor Canola holds it up by the feet and slaps it over and over as if preparing a slab of meat.

"Tenderize her!" he yells.

Or maybe: "Aspirate her!"

Or: "Respirate her!"

The light jangles. Metal shapes collide. The blue cord is cut. The heel is lanced.

"Poor little thing!" somebody shouts next to my ear.

Doctor Canola dictates: "Tufted head. Yellow eyes. Skin exhibits chitinous scaling. Genitals ambiguous. Observations at birth consistent with Strigiformes—"

Nurse Clipboard writes it all down. Doctor Canola thinks he's speaking a special kind of doctor-speak that is not audible to me, the patient. In spite of his assumption I hear him quite well. Doctor Canola senses me listening, and he whips his head around and looks at me.

"It's a girl!" he shouts.

I lie on my back, my head coagulating.

I want to hold my girl, but they rush her away.

Doctor Canola is smiling at me from behind his surgical mask. He is seeking to distract me from the missing baby. I lose trust in him completely.

"This will calm you," Doctor Canola says.

They inject me, with malice.

As soon as they inject me, I begin to dream. I know I'm dreaming because even though I'm still in the delivery room, I have risen to the ceiling, from where I have a bird's-eye view of Doctor Canola. From this angle I see the doctor from an entirely new perspective. I no longer see him as a malicious and crafty person. I see him as he sees himself: as a good and considerate person; as a person who went to medical school because he wanted to help people. He has just injected the woman on the table with a powerful sedative to stop her rising hysterics. Now the good doctor gazes down at this new, tragic mother etherized upon the table. His eyes are soft. He looks as if he's gearing up to bless this woman. But instead of blessing her, he exits the delivery room briskly, and removes his scrubs, and continues on with his day. That afternoon Doctor Canola performs two cesareans plus one more vaginal birth. He sends a woman home after determining that she's having Braxton Hicks contractions. He does an hour of paperwork in his office, for insurance purposes, after which he meets with a drug company representative, who gives him many free samples of a new barbiturate.

Doctor Canola goes home promptly at the end of his shift. It's like any other day, except, that evening, the doctor is distracted by an unfamiliar feeling when he embraces his lover. The feeling is something like fear, but it isn't fear. It's more like an acknowledgment that he is going to die one day. Of course, as a doctor, he sees people die all the time. But just now Doctor Canola is feeling preoccupied with the idea of death. He can't stop thinking about how his body is not much more than a bag of water, waiting to be broken.

All of his morbid preoccupations, Doctor Canola suddenly realizes, are the fault of that first, hideous baby he delivered in the morning. He can't put that baby out of his head. Doctor Canola finds himself thinking: "That baby would be better off dead." It rattles him to hear his own thought, his death-wish for an innocent baby. He is a healer. He has never once considered passive euthanasia as an option after an anomalous birth. But now he finds himself wondering why it is that he tries so heroically to save each and every child, no matter how grotesque or incomplete the child may be. Are the parents grateful for his efforts? Or do they hate him for the rest of their lives, for the way he left them with a child who will never love them, and who will drain their resources and leave their lives more diminished and unhappy? Does a baby like that even know it is alive? Wouldn't it choose to put itself out of its misery, if it could choose?

His lover interprets the doctor's mood as a coldness between them.

"What did I do now?" his lover says.

Doctor Canola can't explain. He doesn't have the words. He's grateful for the distraction when the two of them stumble into an unrelated argument instead.

My bird's-eye dream comes to an end when a harsh interrogative light shines in from a little window next to my bed, and another kind of dream begins. I'm intensely annoyed by life. I'm very tired. I feel as if someone just disemboweled me. But I climb out the window and begin to walk along because that's what's expected of me in this dream. It's raining and miserable outside, and the only sound I hear is the distant droning engine from a plane with the resonance of a B-17 bomber. I come to a woman painting daisies on her mailbox. When I think back on our former encounters, I decide that I have no interest in engaging her in conversation. I can tell from her posture that the woman is weary with the weight of the world. All of her colors are running in the rain, but I have no sympathy to spare for her, alas. This time the little dog is limping around in anxious circles on the woman's sodden lawn, and when he sees me, he comes over despondently, stiff-legged and with his tail drooping. He drops his red ball at my feet with tired jaws, and then he lies down on the wet ground and whimpers.

I pick the ball up and hold it in my hand.

"What do you want from me?" I ask the dog.

The dog perks up. The rain stops. The sun comes out. The woman goes on painting.

"It's time to tell," the dog says.

The dog begins to trot briskly in a certain direction, looking over its mangy shoulder to see if I follow; and I do follow. Hours pass, or years. We walk and walk, but I'm never tired. The trees grow more gnarled and the thicket more tangled, and the sky grows dark, but the moss on the trees is bioluminescent and lights our way, and finally we come to the edge of all things, where the gleaming meets the gloaming. I follow the dog right over to the other side. The trees here seem to know me. They bend and sway as if to welcome me. I notice that the dog isn't a dog at all. It's a small wild thing, like a fox or a bandicoot of some kind. And then I remember that I've come this way before, many times. I begin to run, and so does the bandicoot. The trees grow larger, and older, and more affectionate. I'm filled with elation. At last we come to the stone path of my childhood. I feel the familiar sense of welcome. I recognize every one of the all-day permanent spring tulips in the yard. The bandicoot, tired from its trials, runs up the front path gratefully and scratches at the door.

The Bird of the Wood opens it.

I rush toward her and she enfolds me in her mother-arms.

Everything is exactly the way I remember it. Her house is made of sticks. There are chickens and geraniums in the courtyard. There are papier-mâché parrots perched in potted trees. My room is just the same. The walls are painted sunset orange, and there are two little beds in the room, with spring-green blankets spread across them. I flop on the bed that was once mine, long ago. I'm too overwhelmed with my own jangled thoughts to do otherwise.

The Bird of the Wood has followed me into my room, and she strokes my head with her long cool feathers.

"No time to rest," she says. "The water is on the boil. The sheets are clean and mended. It's time to tell."

Her eyes, being slightly crossed, give her expression a hint of sadness, and I know she is about to ask me the most important question of all.

"It's time to tell," says the Bird of the Wood. "Are you prepared to be Chouette's mother? Yes or no?"

"If I say no?"

"Then she'll die."

"If I say yes?"

"Then she'll probably kill you," she says. "Quick quick quick. She needs a mother, or she needs to die."

I've been left alone in this barren hospital room, discarded like an empty cottage cheese container with bits of moldy rancid food still stuck to its insides. The blanket on this bed is stained. The sheets are torn. The room is small. There is no window. I hear rhythmic shuffling and whistling all around me, as if the walls were filled with small creatures on the run. It's time to tell. Before I can collect myself, Nurse Clipboard walks in and asks me what I want to name my baby. It seems I must urgently think of an acceptable name because this baby might die without a proper birth certificate unless I hurry it up. My husband had a name picked out, but for the life of me I can't remember it. And then I hear a soft aria singing in my head, that one from Massenet's unbearably tragic opera *Werther*—"Va! laisse couler mes larmes!"—and tears fall inside of me, hammering my heart, until my baby's true name is revealed.

"Her name is Chouette," I say.

"Shoe-ette?" Nurse Clipboard says.

I need to spell it. She gets it wrong. Soon everyone will be calling you Charlotte even though that is not your name and even though you never respond to that name. I don't have time to worry about any of that now, Chouette, because it's time to tell. I need to find you. I need to save you. Only I can't get away, because as soon as Nurse Clipboard goes out, my mother-in-law pours herself into the room, like a wave bringing in jetsam after the storm has passed, and I'm pushed back onto the bed, flailing. I can't get by. My mother-in-law confounds me with her nervous frantic gestures. She is gasping inward, and clawing at her own body, and acting as if she has just heard news of a catastrophe involving many casualties. And now, what's worse, my father-in-law has appeared by her side, mute and suspendered, his nose dripping in sympathetic grief. Who let them in? I want to call the gendarmes. "Oh, honey, honey, honey," my mother-in-law says. "My son is on his way from Sydney. He knows. He knows everything. He's halfway home. He's probably over the Hawaiian Islands by now. He'll be here any minute. What do the doctors say? Where are the doctors?"

I tell my mother-in-law, never mind the doctors, where is my baby? When my question elicits no usable information from her, I rise up and begin to search.

"Honey, you need to rest, to rest," my mother-in-law says. She tries to block my way, but I slip past. She runs after me at a brisk trot, pulling at my sleeve. I pull away. I increase my pace. I follow signs and spoor. Before long I discover my girl in a plastic box surrounded by other small babies in boxes of their very own. All of the little dears are stuck with tubes and needles. It's a barbarous, savage scene that fills me with rage. "Miss, miss, this is a sterile environment!" a masked person shouts. My poor girl's wings are bruised and battered from beating against her box. She is alone and afraid. I lift off the top of the box and I pick her up. Alarms begin to sound. My daughter's eyes are still closed and she is rooting about blindly and her skin is covered in black natal down. I hold her to my breast and she begins to feed. Soon I'm surrounded by masked people who are shouting incoherently as they work something out among themselves.

My in-laws have followed me in here like stray dogs.

My father-in-law makes a febrile unsuccessful attempt to snatch my baby from my arms.

"I'm the mother-in-law!" my mother-in-law shouts. "This child is my granddaughter! The father is my son! This woman has no right to withdraw treatment without the father's permission! The father is on his way!"

But her son's name is not on the birth certificate.

In the space reserved for the other parent, I have written: *Owl.*

I sign another paper.

They free my baby from her tubes and needles. My baby doesn't die.

They let us go home.

Three

We're home, owl-baby. It's where we belong.

We're home, where you and I are going to learn to be perfectly happy together.

So. This is motherhood. I ponder it. I ponder the lonely, cruel, relentless obligation of motherhood. I ponder the loving, soft, yielding wonder of motherhood. I ponder the mystery of who you are, little stranger, and who you will become. Your eyes are glued shut with vernal birth-glue. Your skin is gray where the black natal down doesn't cover it completely. I kiss the red mottle of your scalp. I love you. I love you. To habituate myself to the idea of loving you, I say it many times. You're ugly. I tried not to think that last thought, but the thought snuck in. It was easier to love you before you were born. I'm afraid of you. You disgust me. I've made a terrible mistake.

I'm your mother.

I chose it.

I love you.

I remind myself that all firstborn things are hideously ugly.

We sit and rock together until it grows dark all around.

At some point, there in the dark, after staring at you for so long, and after it gets so dark in this room that I can't see you at all, you become very beautiful to me, and I say *yes* to being your mother.

I say: *yes yes yes yes yes yes yes.*

Why do I say yes? I'll never know.

It could be of my own free will.

It could be that you've injected me with your little talon. It could be that your talon is dipped in the poison of mother-love.

Already my arms and breasts are covered in small love-cuts.

I accept it.

I'm a mother now.

I hear a heavy car pull into the driveway. Your father flings wide the front door. He has taken a taxi from the airport and rushed home, and he has never looked so beautiful to me.

"How's the baby!" he gasps, and rushes to my side. "How is Charlotte!"

"The baby is fine, what about me?" I want to say, but just then you begin to arch your back, and to shriek in my arms, so I just bite my lip and try to console you with the breast.

"Oh, good God," my husband says. "Why aren't you both at the hospital? Our Charlotte needs to be in the hospital!" Yabber-yabber. We were sitting peacefully in the dark together, you and I. Our mood was bucolic and tranquil before my husband's infusion of frenzy.

Now my husband is pulling on the blanket that is covering your little face.

He is gazing upon you, owl-baby, for the first time.

After taking a good long look, he turns his head away and collapses to his knees. He weeps and shudders.

"Oh, Charlotte, Charlotte, Charlotte," he murmurs.

He stretches out a coarse hand in your direction. Not touching you. His hand hovers several inches above your mottled scalp. Now he lays down his head on my right breast and sobs. Still not touching you. I can feel his grief pulsing through me, and I want to hold him, and to console him, and to tell him how much I love him, and how sorry I am that you're not the baby he expected—but my arms are full of my owl-baby, and I'm deeply confused by the feeling of my husband's adult-sized head rooting about at one breast while I'm nursing a small owl-baby at the other breast.

My husband needs me. My owl-baby needs me.

Our three heads form an equilateral triangle.

We're the oldest love triangle in the world: mother, father, child.

That's the moment when I choose you to be the one that I'll love most, owl-baby.

Because no one else ever will.

Good-bye, husband.

Your father swivels his adult-sized head back to take

another look at you. He tries to take it in. He can't comprehend you. His face is contorted.

Slowly he reaches out.

He touches your cheek with one finger.

It's exactly as if you've been pricked by a spindle.

You fall into a deep, dark sleep.

Your father has spindled you and now you've turned to stone.
I try not to blame him. It was his way of reaching out. His
huge masculine feelings were too much for your small body to
absorb. You're not the baby he expected. You're not the baby
he wanted. You've been sleeping like a stone for six hours.
Never moving. Barely breathing. At some point during those
six hours, your father and I have magically changed places. I
see our true selves flying right out of our bodies, and for a moment we glare sadly at each other in midair before we switch
our allegiances. Now it is I who love you, and have committed
my life to caring for you, and it is he who wishes you were
never born, and who is praying even now that you will die in
your sleep. My husband, so recently my love and your protec-
tor, has become our mutual enemy. Oh, quick quick quick. I
need to wake you. I need to save you. My enemy blocks my
way, his big shoulders like a wall.

"Let her sleep, let her sleep," your father says. "The doctors say to let her sleep."

"Pathetic cruel man," I say.

"Hey. Settle down," he says. "You've watched me call the

doctors. You've heard what the doctors say. The doctors all say the same thing. They say the prognosis is grim. They say: Let her sleep. Let her rest. Let her pass. I haven't shaved. I haven't eaten. I haven't left our little girl's side. You know yourself what needs to happen. It's why you brought her home. It's right for our girl to be at home with us when the time comes. She is peaceful. Let her rest in peace."

I beat on his chest with my fists and tear out clumps of his hair. He takes these gestures as signs of capitulation. He presses me into his chest, and the sweat and smell of him fills me up and spits me out. "Let me go," I say, but he doesn't hear. He's deafened by his grief. The phone rings every six minutes. It's always his family calling and my husband always tells them the same thing: "No, don't come, it's better for you not to come." He cries continuously, to distract himself from his secret plan to let you die in your sleep and then start over with a different baby. All of our neighbors support my husband's plan. They arrive dressed like pallbearers. They sit on our little sofa as if in bereavement. They bring offerings of one-pot meals. Our kitchen counters pile up with layers of rotting food. Why do the neighbors never ask to see the baby? Where are their gifts of precious hand-crocheted booties? Where the soft blankets and silver rattles with my baby's name engraved on them? Where the frankincense and myrrh? Where the sweet small bonnets?

It's nearly dawn when I hear small polite rasps for attention coming from your crib.

Your father, spent from his vigil, sleeps on.

"I'm coming!" I say, and stumble half asleep to your side.

You're not only awake but thrashing vigorously about and banging your head against the bars of your crib. Your eyes are closed tight, just as they have been from birth, but your sightless little face turns toward me instinctively. Your diaper has slipped off and you're lying in your own waste. When I pick you up, you beat on my face with both wings. I sing and hum while you scream and thrash. It's a desperate duet. I cradle you gently. I hum a little hum into your small black ear. Eventually you are soothed. You begin to suck on a claw. I lay you down on the changing table and wipe your little bottom clean and pin a new diaper on you. I use a soft cloth diaper because those plastic-wrap disposable alternatives will inflame your skin condition. Feel how soft it is. Once you're clean and pinned, I soothe and soothe. Now we will nurse together. The tip of your egg tooth is just visible behind your small rosy lips when you open your mouth and begin to suckle. You're hungry and greedy for the breast. Within minutes you need a new diaper. I can feel your discharge soaking through my clothes to my skin. This time, as I'm changing your diaper, I make a terrible mistake and prick you with the pin and a drop of your blood falls onto the bleach-white cloth and you lash out and peck at my breast and draw blood of your own; and now we are keening together, and crying together, and bleeding together. And in that moment you decide to open your eyes, and you see your mother for the first time—and as I look back at you, my darling, so full of wild beauty in my arms, I feel my heart fly out of my breast, and I remember how precious life is, and how pointless.

Such a perfect moment can't last. The eyes blink. The tedium of ordinary time clunks forward. The feeling fades and is forgotten.

Later that morning, after your father wakes, I try to tell him about what you taught me in the night, owl-baby. I try to tell your father about love, and forgiveness, and perfection.

But your father is bone-weary from his death-watch over you, and he is grieving your survival, and you are screaming, screaming in my arms, and my words bend and warp until I sound deranged.

The days keep coming. You keep on living. Inside me is a damp and complex geography, a sweaty expanse of mixed feelings, uncertainties, and regret; and all of those feelings spread out from my body like the vast Serengeti, full of dark and danger. The edges blur. The truth is, I have no idea how to be your mother. I inch forward across the veldt, sightless and limbless, like a worm.

Your father adjusts to his new role as a father by working fifteen-hour days, because he wants to be out of the house as much as possible until he reconciles himself with your survival. I adjust to my new role as a mother by working twenty-four-hour days, because your metabolism is so fast that you'll die if I don't nurse you and change your diapers around the clock. As soon as I pin a clean diaper on your bottom, it becomes saturated with your watery, guano-like excrement. The amount of fecal matter you produce makes it impossible for me to keep you clean. If I miss a spot on your body, you'll be possessed by a frenzy of preening that breaks skin and leads to infection. Soon you have sores all over you in spite of my best efforts.

But necessity is the mother of invention, they say, and before long, I have the idea to repurpose our Le Creuset stock pot, a wedding gift from my mother-in-law, to help me keep your body clean. You weigh a healthy three pounds, about the size of a small broiler chicken, and naturally the stock pot fits you quite well. I put you in the stock pot, and I put the stock pot in the bathtub, and then I run water from the bathtub tap until the stock pot is full to the brim and spills over into the tub and drains away. In this manner the foul stuff spills out and the water in which you sit is continuously refreshed by clean water from the tap.

All day long you splash and coo with delight.

All day long I crouch in a puddle by the side of the tub, holding your head out of the water with stiffening arms.

When your father comes home late in the night, I have apparently just dozed off because I awake to shouts of "God, God, you're drowning the baby!"

I resent it. I resent it very much. You're perfectly fine.

Your head never went under the water, not once.

Probably not more than once.

He is the one who wanted you dead.

Now that I've solved the problem of how to keep you clean, Chouette, I'm ready to return to the problem of how to keep you fed. Your appetites are animalistic and a little frightening at first. You're always grabbing at my breast. Motherhood is literally consuming me, and it's never enough for you. Nursing you was barely tolerable when it was just your soft natal egg tooth that I needed to contend with, but within days of your birth, your jaw begins to protrude, and your lips become sharp and chitinous, and before long my breasts are replete with punctures. What's more, there is something about my areolae that sets you off on a fury of pecking, and instead of latching on, you dive at me like a young bird that pecks at the rosy spot on its mother's beak.

A day comes when you won't accept my breast at all. You seem more attracted to the meat of me. Blood flows with milk. And I've never felt so alone in the world, owl-baby. Maybe all new mothers feel this way, but at least those other new mothers have continual reassurance, from friends and family, that their babies are both adorable and worth the trouble to keep alive. Whereas I am a solitary mother. No one else in the world thinks you're worth the trouble to keep alive. Are you accepting the world's judgment, that you're only fit to die, by rejecting my breast this way? But I won't let you die, owl-baby. We're bonded now, you and I. Once more necessity invents a big idea in me. I think back on your prenatal taste for raw livers and I begin to wonder: Could it be that you're ready to tolerate solid food?

In spite of the warnings from the baby books—books that insist I should stick with mother's milk for at least six months—I take a cube steak out from the refrigerator, cut it into small bits, chew it until it softens, and present these bits to you in my open palm. You devour the steak instantly, and when the steak is gone, you dig into my hand to shred more meat, this time from living bone, until I'm crying from pain and happiness. Oh, my dear, how could your mother be so slow and stupid? You're not a broken thing at all. You're an *enfant de la nature*. You're full of new and fresh possibility. As the saying goes: *L'homme naît bon, c'est la société qui le corrompt*. Fresh-killed meat is probably best, but for now frozen bulk orders from online sources will have to do.

After your meal is done, you fall into a contented sleep for the first time in days. While you're asleep, I search for an online site that sells frozen mouse, rat, rabbit, pocket gopher, and mole, primarily for the pet-snake market. To begin, I order five dozen "pinkie mice"—hairless little newborns—for next-day delivery. Until they come, I'll raid the freezer for meats.

The frozen pinkie mice arrive promptly the next morning, landing with a solid *thunk* on the front step. As I unwrap the package, a memory stabs me in the eye, of a time when I was two or three years old at most, still young enough to be sitting in a high chair, waiting to be fed—just as you are waiting, my precocious little one, to be fed by me. I remember watching from my high chair with razor-like interest as eight baby mice, small and bare and pink, crawled out from behind the pantry door in the home of my childhood. I was so young. I couldn't have been able to count with numbers at that age. But the memory is still so vivid in my head that I can count those eight mice to this day in my mind's eye. The bald pink babies came crawling along the linoleum with a pathetic blind slowness that captivated me. They made their way to the middle of the kitchen, where a patch of sun was shining in, attracting them with its warmth and reminding them of their mother's warmth. Once they got to that patch of sun, they grew confused. They began to crawl in pathetic circles, searching and mewling, because they were hungry, so hungry that they had crawled out from their nest behind the pantry door in search of their mother's milk. Too bad. Their mother had died in a trap the night before. And I remember my own mother coming into the kitchen then, and picking up each of those naked pink mewling babies with two fingers, and wrapping them in burlap cloth with loving, tender gestures, and storing them in our icebox for later.

That's all I can remember for now, owl-baby, because you have just interrupted my memory with your raucous demands. You're calling to me, demanding to be fed. I defrost a half dozen of these pinkie mice in the microwave and give them to you. You thrash and slash and swallow them down. You look up at me gratefully with eyes like dull buttons. Every day you wrench me toward a different world altogether: an older world, filled with wild, perfect creatures, singing in the dark.

Rejoice! After your first few meals of pinkie mice, you're a new owl-baby altogether. Your primal diet has transformed you. Your pathetic hunger-cries have stopped. The continuous explosive discharge of sour-ammonia guano that I had come to expect as "normal" for you has slowed to a manageable flow. Your skin clears right up. My only worry is that, about a week after the switch in your diet from milk to solids, as I'm changing your diaper one afternoon, I notice that you're squinting your eyes tightly shut, and you appear to be straining. I wonder whether the sudden change in diet has constipated you. But just then your beak opens and out pops an owl-pellet of bone and gristle! Clever girl! How surprised and delighted we both are!

In the days that follow, I learn your rhythms. I learn when you need meat. I learn when you need a fresh diaper. I learn when you need to disgorge a pellet. I learn when you need to feed again. There is still so much to learn. Your birth has separated us into two distinct beings, and it has severed our intimate blood connection. When you were inside me, I could hear your words and needs in my head, as if your thoughts flowed directly from you to me through our shared blood-stream. Now you're cut off from me. The air won't carry the signal. Not the way blood did. I need to learn about you all over again.

I begin by making this list:

sensitive to sound
loose limbs
paddle-arms
carnivorous
attacks the eyes
spreads poo
chokes easily

Every day I add more items to the list. Every day I'm alone with you, bathing you and feeding you, and tending to your needs. No one visits us. They are too sad about our tragic cir-cumstance. They would rather not dwell on the fate of owl-babies in the world.

But we're not entirely alone, are we?—because all of these other creatures have begun to creep inside the house and nest in the corners, not just the moths and the spiders but many others, too, birds, bats, and baby pangolins, and they watch us and encourage us, and they sing to us in a minor key; and as soon as they hear my husband coming, they creep back into the eaves, to hide themselves.

I've read all of the baby books by now, but they're useless to me. They tell me that by the time you're four months old you should be giggling and cooing, but all you can do is shriek and screech. They tell me that by the time you're six months old you should be pulling yourself slowly across the floor in a primitive crawl, but you're scrabble-scrabbling along the baseboards as fast as a young raccoon. You've stopped growing. You've fallen clean off the bell curve. I'm not too worried about your stature because I've read that many predatory birds are fully grown at eight weeks, and it could be that you, too, are fully grown, and fully yourself, and perfectly proportioned just the way you are. Every night your father comes home from work and acts as if he's surprised to see you still there and still alive. He kisses my cheek with a soft smack, or sometimes he pats my bottom, and then he goes out to his room above the garage. Once in a while we still have dinner together, but it's getting less often all the time that he comes in the house at all. When he does, he doesn't greet you. He's still coming to terms with your peculiar habits. He doesn't know whether to love you or to throw you to the dogs.

As for me, I've fallen into a silent loving daily inertia of caring for you. Each gesture I make, whether to bathe, or to clothe, or to feed, feels like a daily sacrificial prayer, and the prayer never changes. I imagine myself in kinship with those monks in distant monasteries who are willing members of the Holy Order of Flagellants. To pass the time I tell you stories about my childhood, especially about when I was living with the Bird of the Wood. I shared a room with a little owl who, like me, had fled the world, and had found her way to that place of refuge. This lost little owl was just my age, and she was my best and only friend, and together we lived and thrived in the little woodland house. In my childish way, I used to think that this little owl, with whom I shared a room as well as all my secrets, would one day be my forever-love. I took for granted that, once the two of us were fully grown, she would become my owl-lover and my tender-woman, and that we would marry, and then together we would start a family. The Bird of the Wood took care of us. She cherished us equally. She taught us to hear the rustle of insect wings, and the soft gratings of the leaf-cutters, and the voice of the rain, and the reverberant echo of glacial rocks. Each day we woke to a wild shatter of day-birds. Every night we went to sleep to the snorts, squeaks, and barks of the night-creepers. Our lives were simple and good. We cleaned and swept, and we took care of our pet bandicoot, and we hunted for food, and every night we said our prayers. It was a place where I knew I was loved, Chouette. It was where I belonged.

And I would give anything to take you to a place where you could feel the same about yourself.

But I've forgotten the way.

It's time for the first Annual Summer Barbecue since you were born, and I'm nervous and excited.

"What are you doing?" your father says.

What kind of question is that? He can see for himself what I'm doing. I'm packing a little travel bag for you, with your diapers, and your pinkie mice, and your Le Creuset stock pot inside.

"I'm getting the owl-baby ready for the trip," I say. "We should leave by noon."

Your father's eyes curdle until I want to crawl into a cupboard and close the door behind me.

"You know we can't bring her, don't you, sweetheart?" he says. "She's still so small and broken. Who knows what kind of germs she'll be exposed to? She's frail. She's weak. It's our job to keep her safe."

He's shaking his head and smiling. He's smiling so tenderly. He says he loves me so much. He looks a little weepy. He doesn't look in your direction.

He kisses the top of my head.

And then he leaves without us.

I've been left behind.

I'll be spending the day alone with you. Just like any other day.

At first, I don't feel sad at all. I'm almost thinking it was my own idea to stay home with you. Wasn't it my idea all along to stay home with you, owl-baby? Didn't I insist to your father that it was for the best? In my memory-ear I hear my own voice urging your father to leave us behind. But wait a minute. I never said those things. Your father said them. He poured his opinions into my ear so completely that I can hear his thoughts in my head like they're my own thoughts.

The truth is, I wanted to go to the Annual Summer Barbecue this year. For months all I've done each day is scrape your poo from the walls and wash the blood from my clothes, and I wanted to be somewhere else for a change. You're staring at me from your crib. It seems that you have no opinion. Somehow, without really planning for it, I'd built up a fantasy in my head about this day, though, owl-baby. In my fantasy, all of your aunts and uncles are fighting over who gets to hold you next, and after that they fight over who gets to feed you a meal of pinkie mice. They delight in your precocious scrabble-scrabbles across the floor. They argue about whether you look more like your mother or your father. They can't get enough of you. And in this fantasy I've also brought the cello along. With so many people there who are dying to take care of you, I'll have time to play a little. Your grandfather will perk up from his semantic dementia and ask me to play "Ol' Man River," and he'll sing along, and remember all of the words. Your grandmother will tell me how sorry she is for the way she behaved at the hospital, back on the day when you were born, and before long she'll break down in tears to see how unexpectedly pretty you're growing up to be.

It would have been a perfect day.

You squawk from your crib.

When I don't pick you up right away, you scream and screech and beat your face across the bars.

I look at you. I'm very tired.

Maybe I resent you a little.

Once this first small thought of maybe-resentment creeps in, it acts like a fast poison. I'm sick of you. I'm ready to quit.

You're screaming and hungry, and in need of a new diaper, and in need of more bits of meat from the breast—and to be sure, none of this is any different from any other day, because you're always screaming and hungry, and in need of a new diaper, and in need of more bits of meat from the breast— but this time, owl-baby, instead of doing what you need me to do, I leave you there. I close the door to your nursery. I *let you cry.* I walk down the hallway to my former home studio. And I'm trembling. It's been months since I've opened the door to this room. I've been gone so long that the walls of my studio have grown over with tangled vines. I can see small faces peeking out through the leaves. The floor is covered in soft, damp moss. When I take the cello from its case, it smells like a woodland bog. I hear soft skitterings from inside the cello, and look in: I see a family of wood shrews nesting there, inside the lower bout. I let them be. I don't have time for perfection. I trap the cello between my legs, and I take up my bow and begin to play the ephemeral chaotic yearn- ings of Kaija Saariaho's *Sept Papillons.* Soon the air is filled with the beats of butterflies. They flap and fly, and stretch out their long tongues as I play. They catch the notes, like pistil juice. How weary I am of being your mother! How enraged I am at the way my husband has left me behind and at the way that the whole world has forgotten me! How sorry I am that you were ever born! I will fly to Berlin, quick-quick, before my husband gets back. I'll take my cello with me. I'll leave you behind. Your father can look after you. He can see how much he likes it. I'll play my cello in the subways, and take up smok- ing, and I'll think about you less and less until I'm free. But you're strong, owl-baby. You're pulling me back. You're not going to let me get away, are you? Your shrieks come out from your nursery, rushing through the walls and pouring into me, clashing and clanging, interrupting my heart-yearnings and snatching at my skin and yanking at my hair. I'm confused and distracted by your wild attacks. I forget who I am and what I'm playing. I forget why I've trapped this cello between my legs. My fingers cramp, so suddenly that I drop the bow, and I'm flung out of my chair.

Rats and voles are shrieking in terror from inside the walls.

"All right, all right!" I shout.

All is suddenly still.

I give up.

I walk back down the hall.

I open the door to your nursery.

We stare at each other like natural-born enemies. You've stopped screaming. Now you're making eerie, incantatory warning-cackles. At first the sound grates against my skin, but seconds later something changes in me and in my own ears' tunings. Instead of eerie, incantatory warning-cackles, I hear a tremulous, exquisite *glissando*. It's almost like singing. You're tapping your egg tooth against the bars of your crib as you sing, and the sound of your tapping is pleasingly percussive, and almost melodic, and reminds me of a marimba, or a *balafon*.

Is it music?

Could it be we've found a common language?

It's time we made peace, you and I.

I reach out my hand to you. You grab the tender web of skin between my thumb and forefinger and bite down brutally, by way of reply. And I'm so full of hope, owl-baby. I don't see the cello being your instrument, given your hollow bones. Your lack of soft lips is going to make playing horns or wood-winds a challenge for you.

But maybe a little marimba would work.

Maybe a little *balafon*.

To make up for my disgraceful negligence of the morning, I butcher a large rat that I caught in a "humane trap" the day before and feed it to you. You gobble it up. I've promised to never *let you cry* again. You've nearly forgiven me. We've settled in for a typical afternoon together, sharing each other's company in our own funny ways, when a knock comes at the door. I peek through a curtain and what do you know: Here on my porch stands the woman who is known in the family as the *secret aborter*.

Of all the wives in my husband's family, the *secret aborter* is the one for whom I feel the most affection. Like me, she has felt the cold judgments of a family that sees us both as provisional members. Now she is at my door. She has come by herself. She stands uncertainly, off center and wiping big tears from her eyes. She looks ready to dash off without saying hello.

I throw open the door before she can get away. She takes

me in her arms, and engulfs me in her tears, and enfolds me into her soft-mother sorrows.

"Oh, Tiny, Tiny, I'm so, so sorry," she says. "I was on the lookout for you at the barbecue. I wanted to see the baby. Your husband told me everything. I didn't believe the stories until today. You poor thing. I drove right over."

Her crying intensifies.

"Oh! Come on in!" I say.

After such a greeting as this one, so full of tears and female touches, it feels too unkind to keep thinking of this woman as the *secret aborter*. I wonder if a time will ever come when I call her my *secret friend* instead. The air in my lungs is happy and yellow bright. She's come at a good time for us both, owl-baby. You're glowing and happy after your special meal, and you're scrabbling about on the floor with precocious speed, burbling in soft syllables as you make your swift way toward the feet of our guest.

"Is that your baby?" she says.

Her voice is a hoarse whisper. I know that her question is meant to be rhetorical. I don't think the *secret aborter* expects an answer from me about whether the baby scrabbling toward her is, in fact, my baby. I don't think she's literally waiting for me to say "Well, yes, this is your new niece, who did you think she was, the vacuum cleaner?" or anything of the kind. She knows who you are. She has her hand on the doorknob. I feel a stab of judgment toward her because of the way she is judging you. Her tears have dried right up. She's probably regretting that she didn't wear steel-toed boots. But then I think: Who am I to feel unkindly toward the *secret aborter*, when I, your very own mother, was taken aback when I saw you for the first time? And my heart breaks a little. I can remember a time, moments ago, when I held out hope that the *secret aborter* and I would grow to be friends. Now she's ready to rush right out of here, too overcome by the sight of my child to stay.

I'm so lonely, owl-baby. And I'm weak.

I momentarily forget all about my promise to never *let you cry* again.

"What a shame," I say. "You've come just when it's time for Chouette's nap."

I scoop you up and bury your little face in the hollow of my neck so she won't need to think any longer about how you don't have a proper nose. In my head I'm saying "I'm sorry I'm sorry I'm sorry" to you as I rush you away down the hall. I put you down in your little crib and close the door and rush back to my guest. It's not time for your nap at all. You're already crying, and soon you'll be shrieking and hollering for attention, or you'll need another meal, or you'll finally figure out how to open the door of your room and come scrabble-scrabbling down the hallway and go after the *secret aborter*'s feet, this time with vengeful intention.

But maybe, before then, I can spend a few minutes with somebody who isn't you.

A few minutes may be enough to save me.

When I come back, the *secret aborter* is still standing by the front door, exactly where I left her, and she has opened the door a crack. She's getting ready to make her getaway.

"Won't you sit?" I say.

She can't think of her excuse in time. Her polite habits move her forward. Now we're sitting together on the little sofa. She's brought a present for you. There's a big box wrapped in baby-shower paper on her lap. Already your owl-baby burbles are seeping through the walls. Your calls rise in volume and pitch until it sounds as if a fierce wind is circling the house, making the windows rattle. My guest stares into space. I want to tell her how sorry I am that she couldn't tell her husband about her *secret abortion*. I want so much for her to be my *secret friend*. I want to freely admit to her that I, too, hold secrets from my husband. I may even get around to telling her about my owl-lover. I want to believe that, after the two of us share a time of tears and confession, she and I will hold each other in our sweet, bare arms, and we will find strength in each other, the way secret friends do, and after that, maybe, we'll talk exuberantly about the weather, and then we'll laugh and paint our toenails together.

"I should come back another time," she says. "When you're not so busy."

She looks perplexedly at the box in her lap.

"You just got here," I say. "Please stay."

"I got some pajamas for your baby," she says. "In the box."

She pats the box.

"It's jammies," she says. "It's the kind that come with the cute little feet. You know the kind I mean? With the cute little zipper in front? But these jammies won't do at all for your Charlotte, will they? No. I don't think they'll do."

"That's so kind of you," I say. "What a kind gift. Thank you."

She sits like a fossilized fern: delicate yet stone-like. She's thinking over your stumble-feet. She's thinking about your wedge-shaped arms. She's thinking of your fingers like long sticks. She's thinking that the sum of your parts will never fit into those jammies.

"I should have brought a blanket," she says. "Or maybe one of those hanging things, for hanging above the crib."

She begins to cry anew. These new tears aren't happy tears, or sisterly tears, or even tears of grief. They are bitter tears. They are good-bye tears. They are the tears of a kindly woman who has just run straight into the closed-door limit of her kindliness.

"I don't know what to say," she says, and cries some more.

I want to put my arm around her.

But then I remember my musty emanations, and I refrain.

The *secret aborter*'s visit has lasted just long enough for you to smear poo all over the walls of your nursery. I can't say that I blame you for it when your mother is so faithless. The scent of Pine-Sol soothes you, and I use it now to scrub the walls. As I scrub, you start up again with the same eerie, in-cantatory cackles that you made earlier that day. The notes of your song sound fat and ill-tempered, but not unpleasant. I think I've underestimated you, for sure. It may be a fool's hope, but as soon as your father gets home from the Annual Summer Barbecue that night, I tell him all about your sing-ing, and about the clever way you tapped your egg tooth on the bars of your crib, and then I ask him what he'd think about buying you a little marimba, or maybe a little *balafon*.

"Sounds fanciful," he says. "How is she going to play a marimba? She can't hold the mallets. She doesn't have thumbs. She's behind on all of the developmental milestones."

He's right. He's rational.

"You're probably right," I say.

Sometimes when I capitulate, your father becomes easier to persuade. His idea of what it means to be a good husband includes indulging me now and then, especially when he thinks I'm trapped in the throes of a harmless female idea. It also works in my favor tonight that he's fallen into a gentle valley of guilt about the way he left me home all day. He's thinking that he owes me something. I see all of these considerations pass gently across his brow like soft clouds. I wait for his considerations to arrive at their likely destination. He decides there's no harm in picking out a little marimba for you from an online catalog. We order it for express delivery, and when we're done, your father kisses me good night and goes out to his room above the garage. A few minutes later, he turns out the light. No doubt he's exhausted from his many manly efforts of the day. You're exhausted, too, Chouette. It's been an especially overwhelming day for you. You're already asleep in your crib.

I stay up awhile, alone in the kitchen, drinking my twig tea and watching the spiders weave their webs. At times like these, the old voices resurrect themselves, and I grow restless for my old life in the gloaming, where my life was full of music, sweet songs that made the light hum and the

trees sing. When the wind blew, the tree trunks clapped together, and they sounded like deepest-plummet clatter of
giant wood-chimes. I could fly in those days. I could hear the
earth's heartbeat. Sometimes the sounds pulsed through
the air like blood through living veins. Sometimes the sounds
pulsed through me, and made my body sing itself to sleep and
dream soft dreams. The Bird of the Wood taught me how to
play songs on my hunting bow, with strings of catgut. I could
pluck and bend and warble. I could make the colors come.

On the day when the delivery man brings your little marimba
to the door, I ask him to set it up for us in my studio before he
goes away. You're full of curiosity. I'm full of hope. I pick you
up and put you within reach of the long rosewood keys. Just
as your father predicted, you reject the mallets. I'm not sure
what will happen next. I've been thinking that you might use
your stick-fingers to play the notes, or your scrabble-feet.
But instead, after a few seconds of running back and forth
along the tone bars, you begin to tap out a tune with your
little egg tooth. The clash and clutter of your playing is dissonant and new. Your tooth makes a pleasing staccato tap.
You accompany your marimba-playing with hypnotic, atonal
humming. I'm elated until you begin to peck so hard at the
tone bars that they splinter and then break. It happens in seconds. It's too late to stop you. It's done. I try to stay positive.
The shape and sound of this destructive act had a nihilistic
cold attitude all of its own. I'm reminded of the existential

works of Théodore E Libèr, especially his famous *Rendez-vous 1963*, a lively composition that calls for the performer to demolish her instrument onstage with a chainsaw. I think that's the end of this little experiment. But you've kept on playing, owl-baby. You giggle and swoon. The keys have splintered into new lengths, and they don't play the same notes as before. They're new notes. They're your notes. I try to locate these notes somewhere within the Western diatonic scale, but they don't fit. They're falling in between. I'm not sure I like it, but I listen very carefully because I want to believe in you, and before long I'm falling forward into a sound-world of your making.

My life becomes a row of tiny memory-pearls, strung along a limpid string. Typically, you sleep until noon. When you're awake, I change your diaper and feed you a meal of chopped pinkie mice mixed with raw egg. After breakfast you burp up a neat pellet like clockwork. And then, in the afternoon, we'll play music together. I've decided to call the sounds we make together "music." I play my cello, and you run and peck at your little marimba. I'm never sure whether the sounds you make are intentional or whether they are accidental improvisations—a kind of *found art*. Either way, my days have become tolerable. It's true that if I try to play any music on my own—music I might want to play, independent of your wishes—then you'll fly at me and peck at my fingers and slash at the fingerboard. Bach's cello suites can set you off so completely that you draw blood. You'll usually tolerate the Romantics. I can sneak in a few bars of Brahms now and then, but it's risky. The neck of my cello is nearly broken through in some places by your disapproving pecks. I've learned it's best to follow your lead and to adapt to your tunings. We still clash sometimes, sure. The cello is a mammalian instrument, and your notes are filled with sonic avian shrieking. But usually we find a way to blend for at least a few minutes in the day. I like to think that you got some of your musicality from me. The tunes are different every time.

"Stop her from making that racket, stop it!" your father will shout, if he happens to be within earshot. "Her bones are hollow! She's going to break something!"

I pay no attention to his ignorant entreaties.

When the time comes around for the Thanksgiving Feast that year, I have my arguments ready. I tell your father that you deserve to be a part of the family as much as any of your dog-cousins do. "It's just eleven miles to your parents' house," I remind him. "If Chouette can't behave herself, then you can drive us home and go back to the party without us. You owe it to Chouette at least to try."

Your father doesn't answer. Maybe he thinks the whole notion of taking you to see his family is so ludicrous that it goes without saying. He barely makes excuses before he drives away without us.

I feel like Bluebird's wife, abandoned at home, with a bone for a key.

The afternoon is sunny and good, though, and you and I are together, enjoying the sun in our little backyard with a five-foot fence all around. You've been busy digging holes in the dirt while I drink from a festive pitcher of strawberry daiquiris. I doze in the November Central Valley heat. Lazily I begin to wonder whether the *secret aborter* will ever find her way to my door again. Maybe she will steal away this afternoon from the Thanksgiving Feast and come over to see me, the way she did on the day of the Annual Summer Barbecue. I begin to wonder (with no small amount of bitterness) whether she'll ever deliver the promised baby blanket. I can't really blame her for staying away, though. I know how disappointed she must be in herself, to have tried and failed to be a friend. People always say to themselves, "Oh, I must stay in touch with that poor woman, stuck at home with that poor-poor baby, I will make a point to call on her one day," but the days and the weeks keep coming on, until even the kindliest of people allow themselves to forget their good intentions, because it makes life easier all around not to be bothered by your good intentions.

And then I think, well, if the *secret aborter* doesn't show up, then why don't I just put you in my little car and take you to the Thanksgiving Feast myself? I laugh out loud with the thought, imagining the ruckus we would cause if the two of us showed up unannounced. I don't do it, though. My husband's family would take the wrong kind of pleasure in it. They would take pleasure in the way you made them feel superior, and the way you made them feel lucky to have dog-children rather than an owl-child like you.

So here we are, owl-baby, alone together, when you surprise me again.

First you make a sudden movement of your head that catches my dozing eye. I'm still slightly disturbed by the way you can turn your head right around, the way owls do, and that's why your movement catches my attention.

I see that you're staring at something across the yard.

I follow your gaze.

Small bursts of dust are pushing themselves up explosively from a hole near the fence.

I see it, but I don't understand it.

And then, in a single breath, you glide right across the yard—oh, my baby, you're almost aloft, almost flying—

and now there is an animal dead in your mouth.

The season when I witness your first kill is late autumn, but the day is warm. I have dressed you in a sleeveless light pink cotton shift, and there are little pink sandals on your feet. Blood drips out the sides of your mouth and spatters onto your shoes and your shift. In the sunshine, your eyes sparkle.

I wake from my torpor and leap up and come running to wrench that grotesque dead lump of fur and blood away from you; and after that, maybe, I'll spank you a few times—*pum, pum, pum!*—so that you'll think twice about ever doing such a grotesque cruel thing again—

But look! You're coming running to *me*, owl-baby. You're running to your mother, to show me your prize. You want me to be proud. And how can a mother not be proud of a child who wants to show her mother something? How your eyes sparkle! How happy you are! And so I moderate my first response. I make a spot decision to let you play with the thing in your mouth rather than take it away. The deed is done, after all. That thing in your mouth looks relatively dead, and its fur, even in death, looks clean and brushed. It's not a dirty, worm-infested creature, as I'd feared. It was probably a gerbil in life, or a hamster, escaped from its hutch. A pet of some kind. I feel pride as you begin to feed.

I hear a child's plaintive voice from the other side of the fence, calling: "Peanut? Peanut? Mom, I can't find Peanut!"

I'm terrified that the next-door mother will follow a trail of gerbil-tracks across her yard, and that she is about to peek over the fence and see the dead Peanut in your mouth—

But look! You've gobbled up the evidence in a quick-smick-smack—how clever of you!—so fast that this other mother will have nothing to see, and I feel an unfamiliar mix of relief, and shame, and pride, and hilarity, and awe.

I hear the mother next door say: "Don't worry, Henry, Peanut is probably hiding behind the stove again. Let's go in. It's time to eat turkey."

You crawl up into my lap and ask to nurse for the first time in weeks. And I think that we've come to the end of our surprises for the day, Chouette, but after a few minutes of nursing, you clamp down on my nipple painfully, drawing blood, and then you fly to a corner of the yard, where you begin to give yourself a dirt bath. It's what you do to self-soothe, whenever something new and unexpected happens in your life. What has stressed you? Are you feeling a twinge of guilt, after killing Peanut? Was that the doorbell I heard? Has the next-door mother come over to our home to accuse us of stealing her son's pet and eating it? Is that why you're upset?

I sit tight. I don't want to face her mother-wrath, or to buy her son another pet.

An hour later I regret my decision when I find a note Scotch-taped to the front door.

The note is from the *secret aborter.*

I feel a void of wonder in me, to think that she came to visit us after all.

I open it.

Here's a little something for your girl.
By the way, you're an amazing mother. I'm in awe of you.

See ya,
S.A.

There's a big box on the doormat, wrapped in festive paper and tied with a bright pink ribbon. I bring the box inside and I open it while you play with the ribbon.

She has gifted you with three gifts, just as the wise men did.

The promised blanket. A mobile depicting the Three Blind Mice, to hang above your little crib. A "Cuddly Bear" touch-and-feel book that you grab straight out of my hands and begin to shred to pieces.

It's true.

I really do have a *secret friend.*

Four

Your father comes home from the Thanksgiving Feast full of sudden, uncharacteristic hope because at some point during the feast he had a heart-to-heart talk about your condition with his eldest brother, the chiropodist. As the acting patriarch in the family, the chiropodist has lately taken to giving his brothers and their wives medical advice, and his advice often ranges far beyond his foot-care specialty. Because of the chiropodist, your father has come home imagining a different future for you, a future where you're fixed by *medical science.*

"Given the right parameters, I think she'll shape right up," he says to me. "Don't you think she'll shape right up, once we apply the right parameters?"

And in a swift strong motion he picks you right up off the floor and tosses you toward the ceiling a few times, the way fathers do, before setting you back down.

Later I will look back on this singular event, the one time in your life when your father was so exuberant about your future that he picked you right up off the floor and tossed you into the air. And it will seem to me that this is the moment when our family troubles began: precisely at the moment when your father picked you up from the floor and tossed you toward the ceiling, with exuberance, and hope, and love. After this night your father will never give up on his quest to fix you. He will learn acronyms. He will leave his medical journals lying about casually, with articles in them like "Transcranial Stimulation in Children with Bubo Bubo Complex," or "The Uses of Temporal Lobe Surgery in Childhood Aves Disorder," or "The Promise of Artificial Intelligence in the Treatment of Strigiformes Syndrome."

Some may say you *come between us*, owl-baby, but it's not your fault when we argue.

You're the catalyst, not the cause.

I say to him: "What if Chouette doesn't need a fix? What if she is meant to be exactly who she is?"

Your father looks stricken.

"Why can't you ever hope for something better for our girl?" he says. "One day she might get too big for you to carry, you know. She's wild. She's violent. She doesn't have a nose. People are afraid of her. No one visits us any longer. She might outlive us both, what then?"

"I love her just the way she is," I say.

"For God's sake, I can't understand your conviction that there is no way to help her," my husband says. "Just listen to yourself."

The first thing your father does with his newfound hope is to invite himself along for your next "well child" appointment because he wants to interrogate your pediatrician. I wish your father would leave the parenting to me. He has no patience for it. You hate the way the straps of your adaptive car seat restrain your free expression and you scream all the way there, and your father isn't used to the sound and he tries to shout you down, and by the time we arrive the two of you are hoarse from all the crying, and exhausted, and quivering, and dripping with sweat. I've always liked your pediatrician, who is old and an alcoholic. His spectacles are as thick as thumbs. After Doctor Booze calls us in from the waiting room for your exam, his bright pink face cheers me and you settle right down. Doctor Booze is uniformly accepting of your peculiarities. He is never worried about the way you've fallen completely off the height and weight charts. He accepts that you will always be the best little owl-baby you can be. He's patient with my questions. Just lately you have developed a habit of tensing your body, and arching your back, and more often than not your head will fly back like a battering ram and clock me in the chest—does he have any advice for me?

Doctor Booze nods and grumbles.

"You can expect that sort of thing," he says. "It's the sort of thing that happens now and then. Your child is very healthy and very strong."

You scream and kick him in the jaw and he doesn't mind. He understands how it is. He's learned to anesthetize himself against the more painful aspects of the medical profession.

He takes his time looking you over, and then he pats you on the head to indicate the exam is over.

"You're a lucky woman," Doctor Booze says. "Don't worry, little mother. You're blessed. You're truly blessed. Most mothers have children who will grow up to hate them and to ridicule them, and who will leave home as soon as they possibly can, never to be heard from again unless they need bail money; but owl-children never grow up, and they never leave, and they never learn, and they will always need their mothers no matter how old they get."

I cherish his homespun wisdom. I take it to heart.

"What about her hollow bones?" your father interjects. "What about her yellow eyes? Do you know anything at all about Strigiformes syndrome, Doctor? Why can't she bend at the waist? Why does she still weigh four and a half pounds? Are you a doctor? Where's your license?"

"Not to worry," says Doctor Booze. "Your child is who she is."

Doctor Booze has the rare talent of being able to lull you to sleep, Chouette, and now he is also taking a little catnap himself, while you, exhausted from your tantrums of the day, are dozing in his lap.

"Hello? Anybody home?" your father says.

"I never take no wooden nickels," says Doctor Booze, and wakes up.

Your "well child" appointment is over.

"That quack," your father says on the way home. "I can't believe that quack has a license. That quack must be three hundred years old. Our Charlotte needs experts. She needs specialists. We need to beat this thing. I thought you were on it. I wonder what it is you do all day. I obviously need to get more involved in the *day-to-day*. There are treatments. I've been reading up. Early intervention is key. We need to keep fighting, for our girl's sake."

He's all fired up. A week ago, you were a hopeless case to him, and of no interest at all, and he did everything possible to avoid remembering that you existed because he hated the feeling of being powerless to change you.

But now your father has hope.

He has become your bright crusader.

Good-bye, Doctor Booze.

Once your father is done interrogating your pediatrician, and then firing your pediatrician, the next thing he does is bring home a little "therapy dog," because he's read in a journal that a therapy dog will teach you how to behave more like a dog-baby.

The dog he brings home is a sweet, nonallergenic blend that represents all the best qualities of the dog species.

"Charlotte is going to love this dog, and the dog's going to love her," he says exuberantly. "But this dog is not just a pet, honey. This dog is going to teach our girl *life skills*."

It's not your father's best idea. The very next day I find the carcass. To tell the truth I'm taken aback at how quickly you dispatch the dog. Peanut was no more than a mouthful, and this dog was at least three times your size. For you to have succeeded in killing this dog by yourself, you must have taken advantage of a dog's natural sense of trust toward its master. When I find the poor thing, its eyes are empty sockets. Its innards are missing. Its body is a hollow flap. Your father and I hadn't even had time to agree on a name—your father wanted to call the dog Arrow, and I thought the dog looked more like a Muffin. But here's the stunning part. You managed it all in utter silence, while I was busy washing your sheets and blankets in the laundry room sink. At any rate, there is nothing I can do about it now. The deed is done. I clean up the dog pieces. I leave no trace. I tell your father that the dog must have run away. I don't want him to worry about you any more than he already does. Your father posts pictures of the doomed dog on every telephone pole within a half-mile radius of our home, but we never hear a word.

I've been thinking about sex again, after a long dry spell. It's because of my *secret friend*. Every time I think about her, my body begins to feel like a pennant flapping and snapping in the wind. I'm thinking about what it would be like to be touched, and held, and cherished, because no one has touched me that way for a long time. For weeks I've been feeling a wondrous, fluttery anticipation whenever I think about writing a thank-you note to my *secret friend* for the gifts she brought to our door that day. A phone call won't do. An email or a text message won't do. I need to write a proper paper thank-you note, and I need to send it in the mail with a special stamp attached. I keep planning instead of doing. The weeks pass and still I haven't written. I want to fill each bit of space on her card with secret meaning, so that she can know for sure how grateful I am for her friendship. She is the only one in the world who gave you gifts. I spend a long time picking out the perfect card. On the face of the card is a copy of *The Peaceable Kingdom*, by Edward Hicks. Inside the card I write, in my best handwriting:

> *Thank you for the gifts. I'm sorry I missed you when you came by, that day. Please come again. My girl likes to sleep until noon. If you come in the morning, then we'll have lots of time to ourselves.*

The words I've written are full of glassy music and infused with the soft scent of absinthe. To think that I, Tiny, could write such a message! Already it feels like an adulterous message, although I've done nothing. I think about it for a minute or two, and then I decide that it doesn't feel like an adulterous message at all, because my husband-in-name-only is sleeping above the garage and has technically already nullified our former carnal agreement. I'm feeling guilty about something, though. Maybe the word I'm looking for, to describe my behavior, is *childerous*. I'm committing the thought-sin of *childery*, for imagining I could steal time away from my child, my owl-baby, to be with a *secret friend*.

I tell myself to calm down.

I tell myself I only want a now-and-then friend, and that she probably won't come to visit me anyway.

I find myself licking the envelope shut with a certain anticipatory pleasure.

I've been so lonely.

Maybe my *secret friend* will find some time to visit me one day.

Maybe today.

Maybe tomorrow.

Good news! The colony of wood shrews that had been nesting in my cello has migrated to the bathroom. By the time I discover them, these rapid creatures have already built an impressive nest behind the toilet. I'm thinking that with any luck these shrews will breed and replicate and become a handy source of fresh meat. I can imagine a day when I no longer need to special-order frozen pinkie mice for your diet.

We bathe gently that day, without splashing, because we don't want to scare these small shy creatures away from their new nesting place. When your bath is over, I prop open the bathroom window to encourage the development of a healthy ecology. Within days I'm rewarded by the sight of other species dashing in and out the window and running along the baseboards. A week later I find a nest of mice in the linen closet. I don't feed them to you right away. I let them be, to do what mice do. Before long I can hear an army of gentle patterings all through the night. I take care where I step. Our home begins to exude an appealing musk-smell that reminds me of my own smell, especially now that I've begun to menstruate again. Green leafy vines make their shy way in through the windows. Brown and green runnels of mold fan out behind the wallpapers. Thank goodness your father has moved into the room above the detached garage, or he might have begun to notice these subtle changes in our household. It's as if your home is adapting to be precisely the home you need, owl-baby— just as I, your mother, am adapting to be the kind of mother you need. I'm learning more about you day by day. It's happening naturally. I barely need to encourage the natural order of things. It's as if all of the small creatures who creep and fly into our home are looking forward to that special day to come when you hunt them down and eat them alive!

When I mailed that thank-you note to my *secret friend*, I expected to hear back from her right away. But she doesn't write, or call, or text, or email. She doesn't show up at our door. The weeks pass. I give up. I grieve. But then I find a letter from her in the box. As soon as I see it, I realize at once that she took so long to write back because, like me, she wanted to write the perfect note, and perfect notes take time. Even the stamp she has chosen—a cheery American flag with the word *FOREVER* printed under it—feels like a perfect, secret message. I sniff the envelope. I lick it. I open it. She has written that she wants to come see me. What day and time would be convenient?

I want to keep this note from my *secret friend* forever, but you grab it away and crush it in your raptor-like claw and tear it to shreds.

Never mind.

I write back. I'll need this note to be just as perfect. It feels as if my *secret friend* and I are living in olden times, when lesbian ladies sent private notes to one another, and their notes were delivered by white-gloved manservants on burnished-silver trays.

I invite her to come see me. I name the date.

On the night you were conceived, your father made love to me. He might have sensed my loneliness that night, because when we were done making love, he was filled with a sudden terror that he didn't understand me at all. He apologized to me for not loving me better. He stroked my skin with his spatulate fingers, and he wept into my hair. I imagine that he was feeling the emptiness that comes sometimes, just after lovemaking, when a man yearns to feel close to his partner and instead feels the chasm. "How can I love you better?" he said to me; and: "Will you always love me?" That night he was so tender and so sad, and so loving, that I began to have faith that he and I would one day become true lovers, and not just superficially tethered to each other by law, or by habit, or by skin-deep appearance. But just when I began to share my true heart with him, he fell asleep. I realized that all of the loving words he'd said to me just after our lovemaking were nothing more than his self-reflective doubts about his manliness, triggered by his worry that he might not have satisfied me sexually. I wondered if I'd married a man who didn't know that women have interior lives. I felt all alone in the world, and my soul was screaming out for tender relief. Just then a gust of some familiar, gamey scent hit me in the face. It eddied and swirled around my spirit. I felt a soft tender stroke on my forehead, barely there. I lay on my back and waited for the next thing to happen, and moments later I heard a soft melodious voice speaking out from the dark, and the voice said: "Oh, why do you look so sad?" A memory opened in me like a treasure-chest, and I knew it was the voice of my beloved owl, my very own childhood friend. In a flash I remembered everything I'd forgotten about my life in the gloaming, and how we had grown up together, and how, as young children, we had pledged our love to each other. My sorrows overwhelmed me. I had abandoned my dearest owl-friend so completely that I'd left even the memory of her behind. But now she was here with me. I felt her feathers brush the tears away. I felt her soft feather-touch flutter all over my skin. I felt her forgive me. And when I felt her pointed feathers asking permission to penetrate me, I gave her permission, and she ripped me open and rapture spilled out.

A shaft of moonlight shone in through the window, glancingly.

My owl-lover's eyes glinted like precious metal.

"Come away, come away with me," my owl-lover soothed in my ear.

My husband sighed in his sleep.

My owl-lover turned her attention to my husband's sleeping form.

"Do you want me to gut him?" she said. "To pluck out

his eyes and slash his throat and to unbind you from his flesh?"

She waited for me to say the word, and I was ready to say it, but just before I made up my mind completely, my husband's arm fell across me. My owl-lover's feather-wing retreated as if from a poisonous upswelling. My husband woke up a little, then, and without opening his eyes he murmured, "What's going on? Why are you crying, Tiny?" and he pulled me closer, and held me in his arms with all the love that he could manage. I felt that I must love him. He was my husband. His arms around me felt strong and warm. My owl-lover sensed this foreign affection in me, and she flew off silently, back into the gloaming, to grieve and rage at my betrayal, and to leave me to him.

And now I am the mother of an owl-baby.

And it is in such small slips of thought, too short even to be called decisions, that our lives are hollowed out and take shape.

I wake up one morning with a hush-whisper happy feeling in my breast. I don't remember at first why I should be feeling so happy. But then I do remember: Today my *secret friend* is going to visit me. She isn't exactly on time. I almost give her up, but then I hear a boisterous kick on the door, and here she is. What's going to happen next? Since you are on a crepuscular schedule these days, owl-baby, I can count on you sleeping until noon. My *secret friend* and I will be alone until then. What will we do together? After so many days of a life unspooling in predictable happenings, one day after another when nothing ever changes, this new thrill of not knowing what will happen next is almost too much for me to bear. I don't really know much at all about my *secret friend*. I don't know why she's here. Maybe she wants to exchange recipes. Maybe we'll talk about what it means to be alive. Maybe we'll argue about which TV shows are worth watching.

We don't do any of those things.

She checks to see the curtains are fully drawn, and then she kisses me.

It's a friendly kiss. I feel safe and cozy.

The next thing I know she is squeeze-squeeze-squeezing me. Her body is swan-like, but her grip is like a pit bull's. Her pendulous breasts flop and bounce against my tiny breasts. There is a strange abundance of flesh between our beating hearts and I'm not used to it. Without any preamble at all we've come to the point in our embrace where we're about to jump off of a high cliff and into the abyss and I'm not sure I'm ready.

She stops kissing me.

We're engulfed in silly laughter.

"I've wanted to do that since I first saw you," she says. "It was love at first sight."

But I don't want to think about her loving me at first sight, because she first-sighted me on the day I married my husband. Thinking now about my husband, on our wedding day—even if he has been sleeping in the room above the garage for over a year—makes my head fill with uneasy guilty rumblings. I don't have time to ponder my guilty rumblings, though, be-cause my *secret friend* and I have moved on lurchingly from silly laughter to giddy sighs. The pace of our encounter feels completely out of control, and I'm a little scared of her.

"I've never seen your house. Will you show me?" she says.

I can't take her through the kitchen because of all the dirty dishes. I can't show her the nursery, either, since my owl-baby is sleeping there and my *secret friend* is afraid of my owl-baby. I don't want to show her my former music studio because if I open that door, it will bring up all kinds of com-plicated feelings in me. The guest bathroom won't do because it's inhabited by wood shrews. I have no other choice, and so I take her straight to the bedroom. She kicks off her shoes and hops in. She pulls the coverlet right up to her chin and she begins to undress, under the coverlet, throwing out items of clothing one by one. After shedding her socks and blouse and slacks, she begins to toss out the more intimate items. Dust motes float through my line of sight. I can smell my husband's shaving cream. A single ample breast comes peeking out from beneath the coverlet and I can't stop looking.

"Come on, come on!" she says, and pats the bed.

Her glee reminds me of a drunk person. I can't understand how placid I've become. It's as if I'm watching a movie.

Is it a good movie?

Could it be one with a happy-ever-after ending, just for me?

"Come *on*!" she says.

I dive in.

From this day on, I will think of her as my *secret lover*.

Somebody loves me. My hair is made of leaves. My skin is scaled; my branches, sharp. I'm filled up with carnal expectation, all the days and hours of my life. My *secret lover* has done all of this for me, and more. Her love is not a great love. I know that. But I'm starved for even small scraps of love. She even says she likes the way I smell. My musty emanations remind her of the wild days of her youth when she lived in a commune that supported itself by selling composted manure to organic farmers. She arrives nearly every morning at ten, and she stays with me until the owl-baby wakes up at noon. For two hours we behave as if there is nothing in the world except our own two bodies. She's afraid of my child, but that's all right. If I were to say, "My lover makes me happy," it would be the truth.

My *secret lover* makes me confident in all things, even about my mother-instincts. All morning long, when we're not kissing, my *secret lover* is telling me how good I am. She says, "You're a saint," and "I can't believe you can do what you do," and "How do you put up with it," and "You're the best person I know," and "You're so good to her," and "There's a place reserved in heaven for people like you." I feel my soul grow strong. I feel my heart beat more purposefully. All of my doubts and sorrows about my baby's owlness, and about my baby's differentness, and about my helplessness to help her, have grown small and insubstantial. With my *secret lover* here to remind me who I am, I'm strong enough to shove my doubts and sorrows inside a tiny safe, and to put the safe away in a box, far away from my thoughts, on a high shelf, in a distant closet, and I lock the closet door fast with my little bone-key, and I resolve to never think about my doubts and sorrows again.

Now that I have a *secret lover* to tell me what a good mother I am, I'm full of new ideas about how to become an even better mother to you. Parents underestimate what owl-babies can do, and I realize I've been guilty of making the same mistake myself. I've been listening too much to your father, who is preoccupied by the way you keep missing typical dog-baby developmental targets, like *sits alone without support*, when you don't even bend in the middle, or *displays social smile*, when your mouth is as hard as a beak, or *uses spoon to feed self*, when you rip and tear and gorge on food without need of a spoon.

Nowhere in the developmental targets have I ever read: *feeds self by killing small domesticated animals.*

I'd like to see your dog-cousins try that.

Without any real goal in mind, and armed with only the sense of confidence and the joy my *secret lover* has instilled in me—plus the thought that owls, after all, are nocturnal creatures—I begin to take you out at night into the world with me. If nothing else, our nighttime adventures will be a way for both of us to use up your wild energies. We're lucky to live in an exurb of Sacramento, close to hills and the uncut thicket, and near to the once-wild places. On the next new-moon night, when it's very dark, I attach you to a little tether and out we go. You climb up on my back and grab my hair. Together we creep out to where the paved road ends, past the frames of unfinished houses and over bulldozed mounds of dirt and through a stand of luminous birches, where the world turns sudden-wild. There are old mattresses and other junk piled up like badger warrens, where the mice like to nest. There are pools and puddles, where small things gather to drink and to mate. We follow a stream until the ground gets soft and marshy. Then you stop suddenly. You're very still. Eventually my eyes adjust, and I see what you see—why you wanted us to stop here rather than going on: a mother turkey, roosting on the ground with her babies. She tries to turn herself to stone—to not move at all—in fear of what she can sense but can't see. You have brought your beak and talons. I have a little axe in my hand. I sneeze—I can't always be as quiet as you are, owl-baby—and the mother rushes blindly toward us to defend her nest. You give a fearful shriek and hurl yourself at the mother, but she's too big for you and so I help with my little axe, and between the two of us, working together, the bird is dead before she falls over. She's too fat for us to finish the entire carcass, and there are her babies besides. We let the babies be. Some other creature will make a meal of them. On the way home, we come to an irrigation ditch, where I teach you to wash the blood from your face and scales. I watch the way you tip your head back as far as it will go to let the water dribble down your throat.

Your neck ripples.

Today you hunted down a juvenile pocket gopher in the backyard. Your timing was off. At first you only injured it. Its little back legs were broken. It tried to drag itself along toward the safety of a nearby gopher hole, by clutching at the dirt and blades of grass with its front paws and pulling itself along. You hopped along after it, deliriously happy, pecking at its middle parts, until its guts were spilling out. The small thing kept on trying to endure, and to make it to the safety of the gopher hole. You had no qualms about causing another living creature to suffer. I didn't interfere—that would teach you the wrong lesson—but I was wrenched by the experience, and shaken by your lack of compassion. I needed to remind myself many times that owls are not social creatures. You're a born predator. I need to repress my intermittent dog-thinking, and to remind myself that, to be the best owl-baby you can be, you don't need to learn compassion. You need to learn ruthless, solitary strength.

But it was all I could do to not go over there and put the little thing out of its misery.

Now that you've begun to feed yourself, I've been taking a weekly inventory of our household food supply. Yesterday I counted seventy-three wood shrews, two hundred and twenty mice, and eleven rats in the house. I've kept the rat population down on purpose because rats will prey upon the smaller rodents if I let them. A paste of cornstarch and strychnine painted a few inches above the baseboards, where it's out of reach of the mice and shrews, does the trick. There is also a mated pair of voles nesting under the front step, and I add them to the inventory. The pair has just whelped its first litter. I can hear the babies through the baseboards, crying faintly, but I don't count the babies yet in the inventory since baby voles are frequently eaten by their own fathers before they leave the nest. When you first started, you were clumsy. You'd slam into a table leg, or hit your head against a wall, and the mouse or shrew or rat would escape. You kept trying, though. You never gave up. And by now you've grown so agile that you take my breath away. I love to watch you fly across the room a dozen feet at a time and swoop down, and grab, and thrash, and eat. Oh, well, when I say I love to watch you *fly*, I need to admit that it's more of a *glide*, really—your web-wings may never truly allow you to *fly*—but even so I love to see you *glide*, weightlessly and effortlessly, for a dozen or more feet at a time and without a single toe touching the floor. No dog-baby could do that! Very soon you'll be completely self-sufficient, catching three square meals a day for yourself. You don't eat the tails, which is handy for me, because an end-of-day tail count helps me to track your daily diet.

Yesterday I got the wild idea that you might enjoy a change
of diet and I decided to buy a half dozen baby snakes at the
pet store and let them loose in the house. In seconds they slid
under the furniture and into cupboards and hid themselves.
Stupid, stupid mother! What kind of stupid mother would re-
lease competing predators into her own child's environment?
What if these snakes were too wily for you to catch? What if
they went on to devour all the mice and shrews in the house?
The rodent populations that I'd so carefully tended for you to
hunt indoors would be decimated. Worse still was the thought
that came next: that one of these snakes—grown long and
fat from feasting on your shrews and mice—would, one day,
decide to hunt *you*, Chouette.

As usual, I underestimated you. You were fired up, dancing
and scratching at one of the cupboards where a young snake
had just slid. I took out your father's first-press vinyl copy of
Frankie Laine singing "Gunfight at the O.K. Corral" and put
it on the turntable, and I turned it up to full volume to inspire
you, and you quivered with anticipatory bloodlust. You gal-
loped and glided around the house in a triple rhythm, hunting
the snakes down one by one and eating them. Only the last
and largest of the snakes gave you any trouble at all. That one
took a stand in the kitchen. It swayed like a cobra and bared
its fangs, and as I watched you swoop and sway in front of
it, waiting for just the right moment, I heard the tragic, final death-scene of *Carmen* ringing in my ears, the part where

the doomed and lovely Carmen defiantly cries, *"Eh bien!*
Mange-moi donc, ou laisse-moi passer!" and Don José shouts,
"Eh bien, damnée!"—and runs his faithless lover through with
his sword—and then in one stroke you decapitated the snake.
Once you were finished eating its soft parts, you flew behind
the stove. Seconds later you came back with a huge rat in your
mouth. Show-off! Your eyes were aflame with the knowledge
of your power, and you reveled in your fierceness. And as I
watched you eat that rat—the fresh offal hanging down from
your beak—I truly understood, maybe for the first time, what
it means to be a mother. One day you won't need me, Chouette.
It's only natural. The day will come when you feast upon my
liver and fly away, leaving the rest of me for the scavengers.
It's a wonder that any woman ever agrees to be a mother,
when the fruits of motherhood are inevitably conflict and remorse, to be followed by death and disembowelment.

For months my *secret lover* and I have met and loved. We're an
easy couple now. We've reveled together in our shared carnal
joy. We've played silly bedroom games together and shared
our secrets. Every morning I can count on two hours with my
lover, to be cared for and loved. It gives me the strength to
care for you and to love you for the rest of the day, owl-baby.

But just when I've begun to count on my lover's soft affec-
tions, another kind of day comes along—a day that I will later
call the "Day of Tears and Blood"—and everything changes.

As days go, it begins softly enough, with my *secret lover*

knocking on the door at her usual time, and with me running as fast as I can to open the door and let her in. On this day, though, she doesn't kiss me joyfully. She doesn't lead me to my bed. Instead, we sit on the little sofa in the front room, the way we sat together on the first day she came to visit me, back when we were mostly strangers.

My *secret lover* says: "I'm pregnant again."

"Is it mine?" I ask.

She looks at me strangely.

"I love you," she says. "But I'm going to have this baby."

What she means to say is: "Good-bye."

"Good-bye," I say.

But she doesn't leave.

We sit for a while. We're crying for different reasons.

"I'll always love you," she says. "You have made me a better person. You were something new and wonderful to me. But a baby is on the way. You see how it is."

Even after her little speech, she doesn't leave. Maybe she is hoping I'll cry and plead for her to stay. But I don't want to cry and plead. What I want to do is coldly exsanguinate her. After all of my nights and months of hunting with you in the night, owl-baby, I've come to trust my own predatory instincts. I'm thinking now of how easy it would be for me to do her in. A slash of talon. A bite to her gullet. There is no heated passion in my wish to puncture her skin-bag and watch the blood run out. All I feel is the sense of wanting to right an injustice.

"I do see how it is," I say. "I can see that I would have been better off if I'd put my hand down my pants rather than let you into my heart. It's time for you to go."

If she'd gone away then, when I'd told her that it was time to go, then I would have remembered this day as the Day of Tears, and not as the Day of Tears and Blood.

But she lingers, to her doom, because she wants me to forgive her, and she wants me to tell her how much I'll always love her.

Your sleep schedule is all off that morning, Chouette. It happens sometimes. It also happens to be the day when you finally figure out how to work the door-latch to your nursery door. I can tell that you've learned this new skill when I hear you scrabble-scrabbling down the hall in our direction. You're coming swiftly. You sound like a herd of avenging buffalo. My guest's eyes open wide. She can sense the coming danger, but she's rooted to her spot, much like a small animal will freeze in place just before its neck is broken by a predator. My *secret lover* doesn't know you very well. You're usually asleep when she comes over. She's barely familiar with your talons or your talents. She doesn't understand the sound that's galloping in our direction. You burst into the room. Did you hear the cold fury in my voice, owl-baby? Is that why you are now hurling yourself so fiercely toward my *secret lover*? By the trajectory of your small body she judges that you're going for the eyes, but at the last moment you twist in midair and go straight for the midsection and rip her open with a slash of beak and talon. Not really. That's an exaggeration. She's not ripped open. Her entrails aren't falling out. She's lucky to have been wearing her cunning leather jacket. Even so a ribbon of blood is pulsing out in a lively manner through the rip in her jacket and pooling between the sofa cushions.

I stare at the heartbeats made visible with each pulse of blood.

My *secret lover* may have passed out for a moment.

Now she's wide awake and looking down at her wound, and wailing.

Do you remember what happened next, my dear? The way my *secret lover* refused our offer to drive her to the hospital? Outside it had begun to rain. I ran out after her, and watched her weave and swerve down the street in her electric car until she turned a corner. From the crazy crooked back-and-forth of her driving, it looked like she must have been driving with one hand on the wheel while applying pressure to her abdomen with the other hand to keep her insides from tumbling out. Once she turned the corner, I ran back inside to tend to you. I found you hiding in a corner and trembling. All that day we huddled together, listening to the rain on the roof and waiting for the gendarmes to come arrest us. "This is it," I kept thinking. This would be the day when I finally and irrevocably became your mother, and I would love you and defend you to the death, if that's what it came to.

There must have been many car accidents that day, on account of the rain, because there was a reckless abundance of sirens in the air, one after the other, all coming down the street and growing closer, and louder—so loud that we knew the gendarmes would be crashing through the door any minute to haul us off—and then the sirens would doppler away, and move past, and fly away into the distance. It grew dark all around and we never moved. We watched the patterns of rain on the windows every time car headlights lit them up. And still no one came to arrest us. The rain kept on. We heard your father come home late from work that night, in the dark. We heard him trudge and splash down the driveway to his room above the garage. He didn't check inside the house. The lights were out. He probably thought we were asleep. All night long I held you, and you let me hold you. We never slept or moved. You clung to me, overwhelmed by the power of your own instincts. I didn't know how to console you. I was afraid of you, and yet I wanted to be a refuge for you. Soon every bone and muscle in me throbbed and complained and it felt like a penance. All night long I kept blaming myself. By dawn I no longer had any confidence in my ability to be your mother. I'd been the one to take you on those night-hunts of ours. I'd been the one urging you on, and giving you every opportunity to practice your kill-strike. I had been so sure of myself, that what you needed from me was encouragement to be your best self. I had cheered your fierceness rather than teaching you to temper it. Because of me, and because of the way I encouraged your talents, you had happily slashed open your pregnant aunt. I hadn't disciplined you after the Peanut incident. I'd praised you instead. I bought you pinkie mice and served them to you with their little faces intact.

I hadn't taught you at all how to live in this world, or how to be a good girl.

I was a terrible mother.

Just as I came to this last dark conclusion, though, another cadence of a thought came clanging into my head, cutting short my tumult of self-recrimination and contradicting it.

In my head, I heard myself say: "What mother wouldn't want to encourage her child's natural talents? Isn't that what mothers do?"

I considered it.

I decided that maybe I only needed to teach you moderation. And a bit of human feeling.

I needed to make you understand that violence was not always the right path.

But then a different voice in my head interrupted me and said: "Hold on there, Tiny! Won't there be many times in your owl-baby's life when she will need to defend herself against the dog-people? Do you really want to quash that survival instinct in her, and teach her nuance, when she's surrounded by people who see the world in black and white and who look at your girl and see a monster? When the world is full of those who see her as a creature to be shot on sight, or, at best, to be put down humanely? There are people out there, after all, who think that the only good owl-baby is a dead owl-baby— do you really want your girl to lie down and accept it, when they come for her?"

My head argued with itself all night.

Morning came. The gendarmes did not.

I began to think my *secret lover* wasn't going to tell anyone about how you'd cut her open like a ripe mango.

Maybe the gash in her abdomen wasn't as bad as it looked.

Or maybe she was afraid that, if she told anyone, people would start to wonder why she had been in my house to begin with, and then the whole sordid story would come a-tumble out about our *secret love*, just as her intestinal cords might have come a-tumble out if she hadn't been wearing her jacket.

Maybe we were safe.

As for how to be your mother, I still had no idea. My thoughts had long since devolved into a series of horrific, recursive what-ifs. What if you're arrested? What if a police officer shoots you in the back? What if your wings are clipped? What if the protective services people come to take you away from me, after they decide I'm an unfit mother, because I've been feeding you raw animals and encouraging you to hunt snakes in the kitchen?

What if they decide I'm a danger to my own child and take *me* away?

What if you killed my *secret lover* and she's lying in a ditch with her guts being feasted on by carrion-birds and that's why the gendarmes haven't come for us?

As it turns out, your aunt survives. Barely. She loses a lot of blood, and she almost loses the baby, but she comes through in the end.

She tells no one about your attack. She tells no one about the two of us being secret lovers. Instead she makes up a story about an *unknown assailant*. No one in the family believes her story about an *unknown assailant* because she's a well-known fabricator. A rumor soon spreads that, this time, when the *secret aborter* found out she was pregnant, she was so crazed that she tried to cut the baby out of herself with a little grape knife. The lie is too ghoulish for belief and that's why nobody in the family believes it, but it's a damn good story, and they keep telling it to one another until it's almost true.

One of the wives has seen the scar.

Five

After the Day of Tears and Blood comes and goes, your mother keeps looking after you the same as ever, and she keeps picking you up when you scream, and changing your diaper and scrubbing your poo from the walls, and playing music with you in the afternoons. She even takes you out hunting at night, now and then, to look for turkey-babies and other small delights, and it may even look to the outside world as if your mother is the same person, and that nothing has changed.

But everything has changed. Your mother's mind is filled with a cacophony of voices, all crying out the same lamentation: "I'm a terrible mother, I'm a terrible mother." The voices are usually accompanied by Henryk Górecki's *Symphony of Sorrowful Songs*, and Górecki's songs are sorrowful indeed, and that is my mood. I turn up the music in my head to full volume until nothing—not you, not your father, not even the birds that come a-rap-rapping on the roof and windows—can get through to me. Now and then a wily voice in my head will sneak in, though, and try to convince me that I should trust your father, and that maybe what you really need is a good *medical fix.* But most of the time the voices just remind me what a bad mother I am. It's an endless cycle of cackle-gossip in my head that leaves me confused and disheartened.

Your father can tell that I've lost my mother-confidence. Every day he comes swooping in with his next new idea about how to fix you. Once the therapy dog disappeared without a trace, I thought that would be the end of it. But your father found a nearby stable full of specially trained therapeutic horses, to take the place of the dog, and when you didn't get along with horses, your father tried llamas, and when the llamas didn't help you, he decided to forgo animal therapies and to see what Modern Medicine can do for you. He's taken you to see Doctor Zoloft, Doctor Benzodiazepine, Doctor Chelation, Doctor Rectal Flushing, and Doctor Hyperbaric, but none of them have done you any good. He doesn't give up, though. He's convinced that there is a perfect dog-child in you somewhere. He just needs to keep poking holes in you until the holes are so big that a perfect dog-child can crawl right out of your body.

You're three years old when your father tells me that what you need is *swim therapy.*

"It helps nonconforming children learn how to conform," he says. "The child learns to trust the parent, so true bonding can begin."

You can't even walk yet, I remind him.

He waves a hand in the air at me dismissively.

"Honestly, honey, you're such a quitter when it comes to our girl," he says.

He isn't really asking for permission. He isn't really interested in my opinion, even. He already signed you up for a half dozen Mommy and Me sessions at the Therapeutic Swim Center.

"All right," I say, because I'm worn down by his exuberance.

"Good girl," your father says to me. "That's my Tiny. Just you wait. Charlotte is going to love the water."

He's so full of optimism on your behalf that even I begin to hope, along with your father, that *swim therapy* will do you good. I think back on your pre-Cambrian days before you were born when you used to unmoor yourself from my womb and swim around inside me with muscular agility.

On the day of your first *swim therapy* session, I take you into the locker room to dress you in your swimsuit. You like the polka-dots and peck at them, but the synthetic fabric ignites your sensitivities. Soon you're flopping around naked on the wet floor, too wet and slippery for me to grab, while the other mothers and their children look on mournfully. When I try to pick you up, you bite my hand. "That hurts," I say gently. You appear to be sorry. You let me finish getting you into your suit. I carry you out to the pool in my arms. It's a small indoor pool. The space is full of echoes and humidity. The shouts of other children skitter off the tile walls. You suck on a finger and look all around. The other mommies are splashing happily in the shallow end with their babes.

Your therapeutic coach, a man with the posture of a perpetual lap swimmer, is standing on the pool deck shouting instructions through a megaphone.

"Blow bubbles!" he shouts.

Your father arrives, dressed in his swim trunks.

"Here, give her to me," he says.

"It's called *Mommy* and Me," I say. "I'll do it."

While I'm making my way down the shallow pool steps with you, easing us in, I begin to wonder if your anatomy allows for bubble blowing, but I don't get to find out because as soon as your first, longest toe touches water, you begin to scream, and then you pull out some of my hair along with bits of scalp.

I climb out.

"She doesn't like it," I say.

"I told you to let me do it," your father says, and grabs you right out of my arms. Your face is blotched and moist, and so is his. He ignores your screeches and marches down the shallow pool steps with you. You don't like what's happening, but he is the father and he thinks he has dominion over you. Your screams clang from the tile surfaces. Although no part of your body has touched the water yet, you have a correct intuition that an unwelcome surprise is on its way.

"You shouldn't ever force a child, you know," one of the mothers in the water says. "She'll never trust you again, if you force a child."

Her child begins to cry in sympathy with you. Soon they're all crying. Even the mothers. The therapeutic coach is yelling "Sir! Sir!" at your father, from the pool deck, and when your father ignores him, he blows his whistle. You're still completely dry. Your father is holding you up high so not even one long toe has touched the water yet. Then all at once he decides that it's time to crouch down into the water with you, submerging you both up to your necks. You stop screeching immediately. You're filled with silent wonder. Your father is holding you in his strong arms and he's looking into your eyes with fatherly love. You're looking back. The two of you are very still, and very solemn. I have just enough time to think, "Good God, your father is going to pull this thing off!" when you react. It's nothing personal. You want to live and not drown. Your father lets go of you, the bastard, to shield his face, and before I can do more than watch the unfolding scene, the therapeutic coach leaps in and pulls you out.

"I'm her mother, let me take her," I say.

The dripping coach hands you over.

The other babies and their mothers have stopped crying by now. They've been struck dumb by the sadness of the moment. Now your tender little hiccups are the only sound in the place. Everyone is feeling pity for the strange, unhappy, half-drowned little girl in her mother's arms. They're thinking: "What a monster that dad is."

Your father is trying to figure out how to climb out of the pool without looking like he's capitulating to a story line that ends in his defeat.

"Come on, Chouette," I say. "We're going home."

Then your father does climb out, because it's become more ridiculous to stay in there any longer than to concede it was all a very bad idea. He walks stiffly toward the exit. We follow. We don't even take the time to change out of our suits. We just grab our things and go.

A few days after his embarrassment at *swim therapy*, your father tells me that what you really need is a *special school*.

A *special school*, he tells me, is the place owl-babies go to learn all necessary dog-baby skills.

"It's time for our girl to be properly *socialized*," he says. "A *special school* can do that. It's going to be hard for our girl. But hard does not mean impossible. You always pass failure on your way to success."

I just don't know. You're a perfectly socialized owl-baby as far as I'm concerned. After I learned to stop apologizing to others about your occasional unexpected behaviors, I began to realize just how much your natural instincts should be respected. I've raised you to never be shy with an opinion, the way so many girls can be. Your opinions might happen anywhere. In public restrooms. When an unfamiliar shadow falls across your face. If you bite too hard on a stone that you have somehow slipped into your mouth. You have pulled entire shelves of power tools out from the wall at the hardware store. You can knock over long rows of bookshelves at the library. You grab and throw canned goods in supermarkets. You have the vocal range of an old church organ and your voice can ululate up and down the scale from high soprano to guttural baritone, and then you can make your way up and down the scale again, over and over, in a ragged cri de coeur— and at the end of your rages you will run out of energy all at once, and fall asleep suddenly, sublimely, and catatonically.

After one of your particularly memorable rages, and after you've fallen asleep and are gently sighing, and as I'm picking up the glass and strawberry jam from the floor and wiping your poo from the walls, your father starts beating the *special school* drum again.

"There are many excellent schools for children like Charlotte," he says. "The expenses are outrageous, but my parents want to help. Don't these tantrums worry you? Our girl can't keep acting like a wild animal her whole life."

Maybe he's right. But here's the crux of it, owl-baby. Your father wants to fix you, and I want us to love you as you are. I must have some sympathy for your father's point of view, though, because I keep our secrets from him. I never tell him about the time you gulped down Peanut in a frenzy of predatory glory. I never come clean about what happened to the little nameless therapy dog. I never let him know how much I root for you whenever you're being yourself—even if what you're doing is odd, or frightens people, or makes them look away. Your life is one of feces smeared with reckless joy on the walls every afternoon after you wake up from your nap. Your life is one of constant swallowings of things-not-food, and trips to the emergency room to get loose change and safety pins removed from your gut; a life of people staring at you, disgusted, only you don't care about their feelings, because you are laughing, because you are happy to disgust them; and let's not forget the way you reach exuberantly and grab cans and boxes from supermarket shelves, or the way you groan with pleasure when you pull a stack of watermelons onto the floor in the produce aisle and listen to them land with wet, dull thumps.

"Listen! Can't you hear it?" I whisper to your father on one of those rare evenings when the three of us have taken a stroll together in the nascent dusk. You're trilling softly in your adaptive stroller. The soprano-soft songs of birds and the alto patterings of small mammals can be heard just beyond the trees. Living things are diving toward us in the evening light, plucking at our hair before flying off into the dark.

"What? I don't hear anything," he mumbles.

He's lost in thought about how you're not the baby he expected.

I wish there were a way for me to reach him.

"You really can't hear it?" I say. "It's a certain sound. It's the way Chouette sounds when she's happy. It's all around us. It's happening right now. It happens all the time. Haven't you ever been sitting quietly or walking along on an evening like this, when the air begins to vibrate, and then to sing? Maybe you know how it is. You're sitting in the woods, or a park, in partial shade maybe, on a log or a bench. It's so quiet. Maybe there's some traffic, but the sound is far away. You're not thinking of anything at all. You're sitting so still and for so long that eventually everything sounds different. The birds start calling in a completely different way, because they forget all about you, a human being, sitting there in their midst. The insects hum differently. And then, just then, you see something moving out of the corner of your eye, and when you turn your head, you lock eyes with it."

"Lock eyes with what?"

"Something wild and free. A rabbit. A squirrel. A snake. Your lover. Your child. It doesn't matter. Maybe a lizard. Or a bird. Let's say it's an owl."

"What are you talking about?" he says.

"I'm talking about our little girl. I'm trying to say that she's already perfect. She's a small, perfect thing in this world. She doesn't need to change for you to love her. She just needs you to keep still long enough to see her. I wish you could see her the way I do."

He's quiet. He's thinking. My heart leaps. Maybe this will be the day when he begins to understand you. Maybe my husband's face is about to be transformed right now by a deeper father-love, and the three of us will be the perfect nuclear family—oh, how I've longed for it!

"Our girl is not an animal," he says hoarsely. "I can't stand how you give up on her like this. I can't stand the way you make up grotesque stories about her. She deserves a *normal life*."

It turns out to be a challenge for your father to find a *special school* that will agree to take you as a student. Maybe it's impossible. He'll be under the impression that he's found a good match for you, and he'll complete the paperwork, and pay the necessary deposits, and sign the necessary releases, but once the other parents hear about an owl-baby coming to the school, they band together and say, "We're afraid of that child. We're not even sure it is a child. If you let that child into this school, then we're taking our own children out of this school." While you've been known to defy authority figures, Chouette, you would never hurt another child. I don't think you ever would. Even so, the schools hold all the cards. Your father can't talk a single school into taking you as a student.

Just when he's about to give up, your father finds a school where the head teacher agrees to give you a chance. After so much rejection it feels like we just won the lottery. Your father spins me around just like old times and my feet come right up off the floor. I briefly flash back to the old days, before we were parents, when the two of us sometimes saw eye to eye. The school is only four miles away, an easy drive. The head teacher wears floral prints that emphasize her enormous, comforting bosom. Her glasses are broken and taped at the nose bridge because the children at her school are always grabbing them off her face and throwing them on the ground. Her kindly manner reminds me of dear Doctor Booze. I begin to imagine, along with your father, that you'll make friends, and that you'll learn to curb your urges, and that your future opportunities will expand beyond that of apex predator.

Well. I've barely dropped you off when they call me to say I need to come for you because you've been expelled. When I get there, your teachers tell me that you've murdered all of the beloved, newly hatched classroom chicks, brought in as eggs and kept in an incubator for the last twenty-one days as part of a classroom project.

"The children loved those chicks," they say. "And now look."

They've left the entire mess of bloody chick bodies lying there for me to see.

My defenses kick in because I'm your mother and I love you.

"What's the problem?" I say. "Those chicks were destined for the slaughter. They were born to be meat."

They have no sympathy for this argument.

"The other children are traumatized," they say. "They aren't old enough to learn where meat comes from."

Now that I've taken a second look at these chick carcasses, I can see you had nothing to do with it, and I tell them so. These chicks are goo. You would have killed them differently, by slicing their throats open neatly with your talon, and there are no visible lacerations on these chick bodies. Also you would have no doubt eaten a few of them and these chicks are all accounted for.

"Is it not possible," I say, "that one or more of your dog-children, in a fit of sensuous exaltation, picked up these soft warm chicks when they were still alive—barely understanding that these were living things—and closed their fists, and *squeezed* until the bits of meat and blood ran out through their fingers like warm Play-Doh?"

"No," they say. "That isn't possible. It's not in the realm of possibility."

"It's a simple fact that dog-children can be casually cruel," I remind them. "Think of how good it would have felt to squeeze such soft warm peeps through your own fingers, back in the day, before you knew where meat comes from. Children can't be blamed for seeking tactile pleasure. It isn't fair to hold this kind of mistake against a child."

"Animal abuse is a first sign of serious psychological difficulties," they say. "We don't want to frighten you, but we think you should be terrified."

It's exactly this kind of narrow, prejudicial thinking that I've tried to shield you from, Chouette. Frankly I'm glad to learn the truth about this school before you spent another day in their clutches.

It's not that I'm against the idea of school for you, Chouette, if we could only find a school that accepts you for who you are. Sometimes you look so lost and lonely to me. Sometimes I wish you had a little friend, someone who would understand you and who would love you for yourself. I once had such a friend. But nothing ever lasts, does it? Not even the best friendship. Not even the purest love. My own best friendship—my own purest love—ended abruptly, and without good-byes. A day in my childhood came loping, loping along when my dear owl-friend and I were running together through the gloaming, so fast that branches slapped against our arms and faces. Trees flashed by and the air was crackling. It had been raining for days, but that morning it was fair and the air was full of damp new life. I think I had never felt so happy. My friend and I came to a field full of grass, newly grown, after the rain. When the breeze passed through the grass, it looked like rippling waves, and when the same breeze passed over our faces, it made us feel like ancient warriors. The grass was so appealing that without a word we threw ourselves down on our backs in it. Birds passed overhead. Small ghostly roots grew up from the damp ground. Grubs and pill bugs scuttled between my fingers. No one in the world knew where we were: That was the best thing.

My owl-friend touched my hand. Magically our fingers wove together. The balance between us felt delicate and terrifying. I was afraid to move.

A few seconds later my friend rolled over on top of me, so casually that it still seemed like a silly game. I was under her. She was above. Our bodies were pressed together like praying hands. The tall grass all around us waved and danced. I was so content. I could feel her heartbeat pulse in time with mine. She lifted her head and we looked into each other's eyes. Her face was very close to mine. I think it must have been the first time I noticed that she didn't have a nose. She kissed me. She kissed me again. Her kisses were like questions. Didn't I want her to kiss me? I think I did, but I was afraid. I loved the feeling of her breast-feathers pressed against my bare chest. But I had also just seen for myself, really seen for the first time, that she didn't have a nose. I heard my father's voice in my head, shouting: "That's what you'll grow up to be, Tiny-girl, if you don't obey me! You'll grow up to be a monster like your mother!" I was so confused to hear my father's voice in my head, after being free of him for so long, that I pushed my owl-friend off of me and stood up. I laughed and brushed the grass from my skin.

"I'm hungry," I said. "Let's go home."

After that day I began to experience life in the gloaming very differently. At first it was just small things. I noticed that my feet were unshod, and that my skin was cracked. The taste of fresh blood in my mouth, once thrilling, had become cloying to me. My owl-friend had begun to irritate me. Each day her voice became more grating, and her face more repulsive, and her hulking presence more stifling. My friend could sense the change in my mood, but she didn't know how my feelings had changed toward her. She only knew that I was sad. I began to avoid her, and to spend more time by myself. A day came when I wandered alone very near to the border where the gloaming met the gleaming. I began to imagine a happy scene waiting for me at my old home. I imagined our house, newly painted: Instead of the dull-putty color I remembered, it would be a cheerful yellow, and the shutters would be royal blue. The yard would be filled with purple phlox and yellow chrysanthemums. Everything would be very clean and well-ordered, and there would be a new little sister there for me, jumping rope in the yard, about half my age, wearing a pretty little dress and with hair as brushed and shiny as a brass spittoon. "Mommy! Daddy! My sister has come home!" she would shout, and our mother and father, long since reconciled, would rush out with tears streaming. My woolgathering about my future became so intense and delightful that I stepped right over to the other side. I was instantly dazzled. I'd completely forgotten how the other-world was full of color-whorls and always-light. But otherwise, nothing looked familiar. Tall glass buildings lined the streets, reflecting one another in their windows, and the sidewalks were crowded with shoppers. My old neighborhood had been razed to the ground. Everyone was a stranger to me. The light and the bustle began to frighten me, and before I could remind myself of who I was, or of the loved ones who were waiting for me at home in the gloaming, a gallant knight came riding out from the canyons between the buildings, and he said to me: "Little bird, come live with me and be my love, for you look in need of rescue, and I am in need of a little wife."

And he carried me away.

Not one to give up, your father finds another school for you, where you do something so unexpected that the head teacher calls the gendarmes. Once more I'm slapped in the face with the cruel reality of how others react when a child is in any way different from the herd. When I get there, you're in little plastic handcuffs and a gendarme has his knee planted on your chest. I point out to him that you're two feet tall and weigh four and a half pounds at most, on account of your hollow bones. You're practically still a baby. You're literally still in diapers. He agrees to let me take you home instead of arresting you and taking you away in his paddy wagon. The next day the school summons me back to sign some papers. I bring you with me, owl-baby, to remind them that you, like any other child, deserve understanding. The formerly optimistic principal won't look us in the eye. She keeps looking at the Beanie Babies collectibles on her desk instead.

"Thank you for coming," she says. "Please restrain the child or I'll need to call in the security guard. I need your signature on this *incident report*. It's a legal requirement."

She reads aloud from her *incident report*.

"'*Child* made a gesture that her teacher interpreted as hostile,'" she reads. "'*Teacher* took a step back and tripped over a toy truck. *Teacher* fell and fractured left ankle.'"

She flourishes the paper in my direction.

"It needs your signature."

"How can you say that it's *Child*'s fault if *Teacher* tripped and fell?" I say. "That toy truck should have been put away properly."

"It's what *Child* did to *Teacher*, after *Teacher* fell," she says in her calm drone of a voice. "I'll read on, if you like. '*Teacher* suffered facial lacerations. *Teacher* required eleven stitches.'"

She smiles.

"There's more. I've really never seen anything like it before. Not in such a young child. To tell the truth, I'm afraid of your child. You can read the rest for yourself. You need to sign both copies. You take one copy home with you. We keep the other one for our records."

Naturally I've begun to resent her for her petty bureaucratic ways. I don't care for the way she keeps telling me to sign the papers, as if the papers are more important than you, owl-baby. But I sign, because I'm sad, and because I feel defeated, and because all of my arguments on your behalf have flown right out of me.

"Does this mean she can't come back?" I say.

"I wish your daughter the very best," the head teacher says. "I really do."

That's the end of your school days.

Your father moves right on from his many disappointments with *special schools* and a few days later he comes home snapping his fingers and bouncing on his toes because he's so full of hope about his next new idea of how to fix you.

He tells me about *tough love.*

He's heard about *tough love* from a middle brother, who heard about it on TV.

"It's a way to promote a child's welfare by requiring them to take responsibility for their actions," your father explains. "The problem with Charlotte is that you do everything for her."

"I'm the problem?"

"Yes, that's right, you're the problem. Mothers are always the problem," he says. "My brother knows an expert in *tough love* therapy. We should take Charlotte to see him, maybe."

He makes an appointment.

"With less than a year of *tough love* therapy, your child will be an exceedingly well-mannered child, and what's more, she'll be verbal," the *tough love* therapist tells us. "There is no organic reason for your child not to speak like a normal child her age."

At your first session the *tough love* therapist invites your father and me to watch and learn from his methods so that we can practice them on you at home. Your father and I sit in a dark room behind a one-way mirror. Your father is so full of jittery hope that he is holding my hand and he won't stop squeezing it. We have a very fine view of you and the *tough love* therapist in the next room over. You're both sitting cross-legged on a coiled wool rug, and the *tough love* therapist has placed a big steel bowl of Skittles between you. He keeps wagging his index finger in your face. Every time you try to take a Skittles without first saying "please," the *tough love* therapist slaps your hand. The first slap wakes my mother-instinct right up, believe me. If this is how a famous *tough love* therapist treats you, well then, maybe I'm not so bad a mother after all. This *tough love* therapist is a man of intestinal fortitude, and he can keep up his slapping regimen forever it seems. Whenever I try to run next door and put a stop to it, your father pushes me back down in my seat and reminds me that we need to trust the process, until I feel ready to throw my chair right through this one-way mirror and crawl over the shards and rescue you myself. It turns out you don't need me to rescue you after all. You make your feelings known to the *tough love* therapist by biting off an insubstantial portion of his index finger. It's nothing serious. It's above the first knuckle. You gobble it right up, even the bit of bone.

"That's okay," your father says on the way home. "We have many other hopeful avenues to explore."

After we get back from your *tough love* therapy, your father goes off to his little room above the garage, and that's nothing new, but tonight I wish he hadn't gone away so quickly, because to tell the truth, I'm afraid to be alone with you. It's a new feeling. I've never been afraid of you before. I keep thinking back on the pale shocked face of the *tough love* therapist as he stared at his missing fingertip. I can tell by the precious fire in your eyes that you blame me for your *tough love* ordeal, and I can tell that you're not ready to forgive me. That's fair, owl-baby. I'm your mother, and I'm supposed to look after you. I failed you, and I'm sorry. Will you forgive me? Your body is vibrating with pent-up emotion. I have the feeling that you're about to teach me a lesson. First you stare at me, to make sure I'm paying attention, and then you scrabble-scrabble in the direction of our music studio. I run after you, but it's too late. Already you're attacking my cello, splintering it apart—oh, my darling girl, please, no, not that—and now that my cello is in long splinters, you've moved on to your little marimba. You destroy it completely. When you're satisfied that you've done all the harm that you can, you use your little pincer-hooks to climb the drapes, and you perch up there on the curtain rod, glaring down at me. That's right, my girl. You sure showed your mother, didn't you? I'll be calm about it. I won't shout. I won't paddle you. I won't blame you, that is. I won't. You're an owl-baby. I'm your mother. I understand. I love you. And as I keep telling myself these things, the actual truth of the matter boils up in me and takes on the shape of a rage so huge and hot that it feels like blind hate. I hate you. I could fly right up there to where you're perched and throttle the life out of you with my bare hands.

But then, as quickly as it came, the rage drains out of me.

Now I'm just tired.

I flop down on my little chair. I gaze at the pile of deadwood splinters.

My body feels like crumpled paper.

You stay up there on the curtain rod. You're not ready to reconcile. I'm not ready to reconcile, either. The two of us sit in vigil through the night, with the corpses of our former loved ones lying cracked and dead upon the floor. We're saying good-bye to something we once shared. We're at a wake. We're in mourning.

That is, I'm in mourning, owl-baby, and now and then I still like to think that you're feeling what I think you're feeling. But I can't really tell what you feel. I don't know anything.

The days and weeks and sighs keep coming. I take care of you. I change your diapers. I clean up your pellets and wash the walls. I try to focus on the "ups" in life. You help me. If I don't smile enough, you peck at my eyes and throat, until the only choice I have is to see your point of view, and to accept the inevitable, and to be happy with my lot.

But your father isn't happy at all. His frame is gaunt. His shoulders are cramped. His eyes are aflame with maniacal conviction.

"What's going on with you?" I say.

He smiles a soft smile.

"What if I told you the doctors are *this close*?" he says.

He holds up his thumb and index finger so there's just a sliver of space between them. He's been holding up his finger and thumb in precisely this gesture for years now, nearly as long as he's been a father.

"You wouldn't care if the doctors were *this close*," he says, and laughs a little. "It wouldn't matter to you one bit. You'd fight me, even if I told you there's a way to fix our girl so that she can have a nearly normal life. We won't be here to take care of her forever, you know. We're going to die one day. Modern medicine is discovering ways to help children like our child every day, and one day you're going to see how right I've been. Oh, holy Jesus, honey, don't you long for the day when our girl can hug us back? The day when our girl can finally tell us that she loves us?"

All the time he keeps saying to me: "She needs to learn."

You don't need to learn anything.

He's the one who needs to learn.

And you're the one who, one day, will teach him.

I begin taking you to play at the neighborhood park every afternoon, to fill up the empty time when you and I used to play our music together. Today I'm sitting in my usual spot on a bench where I have an excellent view of you as you climb and play. I have nothing better to do than to sit there, because my *secret lover* has abandoned me, and your father can't stand the smell of me, and the music that you and I used to play together has come to a violent end. Before too long I begin to woolgather. It's an old habit that I've tried to stamp out since becoming your mother, because whenever my attention wanders away from you, some crisis or another is sure to follow. The air is damp from rain that fell the night before and there's a puddle by my feet. I've fallen into that fragile mood that comes over me sometimes when I begin to feel sorry for myself. The puddle by my feet is nothing special. It's a collection of water that has nowhere to go, just like I have nowhere to go. But see how the water reflects the variegated light as the clouds curl over it; and a leaf has fallen in, and the leaf is gently resting on the surface of the water, like a small boat ready to carry a traveler off to the far shore. A small breeze springs up and ripples the water so it vibrates, and the leaf and its traveler are sent on their way. Soon I'm pondering the way beauty is always right in front of us to be discovered, even in the most circumscribed spaces. Even in my own little life. Even if I were to become rooted to the ground, right now, with my neck so hard and wooden that I'd have no way of looking in any other direction except to stare at this little puddle, my life would be rich indeed. I would think these thoughts. I would watch the sun go by, and then the moon.

The air is fresh from last night's rain.

I breathe in and out with contentment.

It's just a few seconds of distraction, but it's enough. I hear screaming. I know at once that this screaming has something to do with you, and that by letting my attention wander from my only task, which is to look after you, something has happened. I know even before I turn my head that you have attracted the attention of the dog-people, and that they are gathering against you with sticks and stones—oh, my darling!—and my body reacts, and I run to rescue you.

But I'm wrong.

Because, here you are, perched high on the play structure,

at the very top, and you're clutching the bars and gurgling with joy and smiling down at life's passing parade.

A little boy has fallen somehow. He lies flat on his back, not moving.

"I can't feel a thing," the little boy keeps saying. His voice is a tight little bleat.

No one saw how the accident happened.

A woman, a mother, keens over the boy.

"Don't move him!" a helpful voice cries from the crowd. "I'm a doctor! Let me see him!"

The doctor's officious shouts frighten you down from the bars, and you come scrabbling in my direction. I take you back with me to our favorite bench, where you settle into my lap. A few minutes later, a woman sits down on the bench next to us. She is dressed in a severe blue suit. She seems content, like us, to watch the passing parade. "Can you feel this, little boy?" the doctor says, and pinches the boy's toes— "How about this?"—and the mother of the injured boy keeps crying inconsolably until her cries charge the air with such confusion that you begin to scream, owl-baby, and before I know it, as quickly as that, this woman in the blue suit who is sitting on the bench with us scoops you up from my lap and begins to dandle you on her knee.

"Stop, please, give her to me," I say.

I'm afraid of what you might do to her.

Only, look: You've stopped crying in this woman's ample arms. You haven't calmed down this quickly since I first fed you pinkie mice. I grow all the more astonished when this stranger-woman begins to praise you.

"Glory, glory," she says, and "Mother, there is something *holy* and *perfect* about this child," and "How lucky you are to be her mother," and "I can tell that this child is touched by God."

She looks with loving compassion into your yellow-saucer eyes while you suck softly on one claw.

You gift her with one of your rare smiles.

"You should come to our Sunday Service," the woman in blue says. "You should bring your little babe along. Our pastor will bless her. Come this Sunday, if you can. We can even baptize her, if you like."

I conclude, with bitterness, that this woman's kindness must have been prompted by her ulterior motive of saving souls.

"I'd love for you to meet our pastor," the proselytizer says.

She hands you over, and she fishes a pamphlet out of her breast pocket and hands it to me.

"Our pastor is a good man," she says. "You'll like him. There will be other mothers to meet."

My heart is full of questions.

Maybe you should be enough for me, Chouette, but I'm lonely. I just am. Even if my last relationship ended in tears and blood, I keep thinking about how nice it would be to have a friend of my own. This new friend of mine wouldn't need to be a musician or even a *secret lover*. I would be satisfied with a gin rummy kind of friend. Or any friend. I begin to think back on the proselytizer in her severe blue suit, the one we met at the park the other day. I think about the way she dandled you on her knee and you didn't mind. Maybe I could find a friend for myself at her church. People of faith like to believe that we are all equally beloved of their God. Maybe they'll think that you, too, are equally beloved of their God, owl-baby. I decide it won't do any harm to go there on a Sunday morning, to see for ourselves.

You've damaged the inside of my car to the point where it's impossible to drive, but I convince your father to drive us to the church while I hold you in my lap. I keep you as calm as I can for the journey. I want you to make a favorable impression on these good people so that they'll invite us back another time. My husband doesn't see the harm in us going to church because he has no idea about the power of faith. When it comes to God, he is one of those superior sorts of skeptics. On the way he keeps up a running patter of yabber-yabber from behind his odor-absorbing face mask. A side benefit to his yabber-yabber is that the sound of his voice keeps you distracted and happy, and not on the attack.

Your father lets us out at the curb.

He tells me to call him when it's over.

As soon as we step out of the car, the woman in the severe blue suit materializes by my side, and I think: Yes. This is going to work. This church is going to change my life.

The woman's face is radiating joyous goodwill.

"Welcome, welcome," the woman says.

I don't think she remembers us. Before I can remind her that we met before, though, a host of other women descends on us as if from heaven to proclaim: "Glory, glory be, what a lovely little baby, what a little angel she is." You look beatific, and the proselytizers say so. The women herd us in through the tall oak doors. They seat us in front, with all the other mothers of special babies. Before the service begins, we mothers show off our wounds and ragged scars to one another, and we touch one another's sorry breasts. I love being in the company of these other mothers, who all have special babies of their very own. These mothers won't blame me for my owl-baby's tantrums, and won't think twice about my owl-baby throwing feces or regurgitating pellets or chewing the epistles or eating the small grubs that she digs from the ridged wooden grooves in the pews. These women are my soft sisters. Each of us knows from experience that birthing any child is the start of a lifelong terrorization by the very child we love, and yet we mothers are able to bear it because we love our children more than we love our own lives, even as our children blithely seek to destroy us. We mothers are tragic in the same way exactly. That said, you're the most special baby here by a long shot, owl-baby. It's not even close. That's probably why we're given the place of honor, front and center, where we have a commanding view of the enormous stained glass window behind the altar. The window depicts a standard contemporary rendering of a risen Christ with a little dove in his hand. There is an enormous and deep baptismal font in front of the altar—enormous enough and deep enough to submerge a grown person, which leads me to believe that baptism is a cherished ritual among these people. The people file in. The organ sounds. The organist suffers from scoliosis, and her reading glasses make her eyes look enormous.

The choir begins to sing:

> My Shepherd, you supply my need,
> Most holy is your name;
> In pastures fresh you make me feed,
> Beside the living stream.

The pastor emerges from a secret door. He is large and barrel-chested, and his voice thunders out in a bass-baritone range, so resonant that it makes my skin tingle and my ears ring.

He hoots from the pulpit.

"When you give a feast, invite the poor, the lame, and the blind, and you will be blessed, because they cannot repay you," he says.

There is call and response. There is weeping and rejoicing. There is singing and quiet contemplation. There is wonder and jubilation.

"Take me and eat me," the pastor says, and you grow so excited by these words that you strain toward the pastor and I need to lock my arms to keep you safe in my lap. Eventually you settle down and amuse yourself by pecking at my buttons, and I think maybe it's going to be okay. Maybe we can learn to fit in, Chouette. Maybe you'll find a friend among these other special children. Maybe I'll make friends with a mother.

The time comes for me to bring you to the altar and to offer you up for a blessing. The pastor anoints you with oil.

As he rubs the oil on your head, I can hear your thoughts as clearly as if you were talking out loud. It's miraculous. In your head you're saying: *Warm and light. Cold and red. Claws like snow. I skip. I trip. I chirrup. I crush and kill and rip.* Your thoughts lack semantic clarity, but they fill me with joy because it's the first time I've heard your inner thoughts so clearly since you were in the womb, clamoring for frozen chicken livers. I'm prepared to be persuaded that religion is good for us both. But then the people crowd in and begin to pray aloud and to put their hands on you, and after that they want to plunge you into the baptismal font, and your thoughts become jittered and unhappy, and the scene feels strange, and unnecessarily intimate, and I'm uncertain again.

In the end I decline their generous offer to baptize you.

After the service is over, we all eat day-old donuts together in an oblong yellow room in the basement and drink coffee dispensed from a giant percolator. You are subdued, almost soporific. I wonder whether your calmness is because of all the blessings you received that morning, or if it's an aftereffect of the very large meal of pinkie mice you ate the night before. One of the kindly blue-suited women who first greeted us on the curb now offers to drive us home. You've been exceedingly well behaved so far that day, and I've been influenced by the talk of the Lord's forgiveness, and so I risk accepting her offer. On the way home you grow unnerved by the woman's tentative driving, and upset by the way she tends to brake for no reason in the middle of the block. After a particularly irritating jolt of the brakes, you peck at my arms so fiercely that I lose my grip. I let go of you, and you fly straight at the kind woman and make a stab for her soft parts. Although the kind woman's eyes are perfectly fine in the end—you only succeed in digging a shallow gash along her temple—she overreacts in an ignorant way, running her car up onto the curb, and after that she ends up abandoning us by the side of the road. I need to call your father to come get us. I'm sure that once this woman tells her gossipy, exaggerated side of things to the others we will no longer be welcome at Sunday Service. The entire episode—how it began with ebullient gestures of love and welcome, and ended ignominiously with the two of us dumped by the side of the road—leaves me feeling cynical about religion, and I resolve to never again be taken in by those who offer friendship to me, and acceptance of you, merely as a way to feel good about themselves.

After the *tough love* setback your father enters into a state of continuous, waking frenzy about you. He thinks time is running out for him to save you. In just the last few months he's taken you to see Doctor Lupron, Doctor 420, Doctor Bleach Cleanse, and Doctor Transcranial Magnetic Stimulation. There are doctors and more doctors, and after that there are pseudo-doctors and proto-doctors and not-a-doctors for you to see. There are specialists and super-specialists and so-called specialists, and anytime I try to intervene, he accuses me of not caring, and reminds me of my faults, and drills his ideas into my head until I go along with them.

A week before your sixth birthday, your father tells me that he's made an appointment for you to see a great new doctor who has opened a treatment center for owl-babies in Malibu.

"What makes this doctor so great?" I say. "What's this one's specialty?"

He's vague about it.

"I'm not sure you need to understand all the ins-and-outs of Doctor Great's procedures, honey," he says casually. "He's the leader in his field. That's what you need to know. His field is taking care of children like our child. He normalizes them, that is. He's renowned. He's in all of the journals. The children he treats are transformed. They're leading nearly normal lives!"

My hopes are dashed. He hasn't mentioned new doctor appointments for a few days and I'd been thinking that he was settling down a little. He's in a fugue state where all of the fear and disgust he feels toward his owl-child have been quelled momentarily by hope. He shoves his phone in my face.

"Look at Doctor Great's website! Look at these pictures! Look at all these children!" he says. "They're getting better! They're almost normal!"

I take his phone and look.

It's true. The website has many before-and-after pictures of owl-children. The pictures span the years. I touch one picture, the one of the child who looks the most like my own baby. The child in the photograph begins to smile. It's the first human touch the poor kid has felt in decades. Before I know it, I fall right into the picture. I can see your father yelling down at me from the ceiling. His face is huge. It's as if your father is inside a ceiling-sized jumbotron. Your father is in living color, but down here in the photograph I'm grainy black-and-white, and I'm wearing a girdle, and my hair is styled very much like Veronica Lake's hair in the classic World War II film *So Proudly We Hail*. I deduce from these clues that the picture I've fallen into is from that era. I next observe that I'm in a medical setting of some kind, possibly an examination room, and there is a nurse with me in this scene, spankingly dressed in a nurse's uniform, complete with white cap and white shoes. The nurse is holding an owl-baby down on a steel table, and there is also a doctor in the room with us, and the doctor is poised to plunge a giant syringe into the squirming owl-baby's exposed breastbone.

"Hand her over, you monsters!" I yell.

Needless to say they are surprised to see me.

I wrestle the owl-baby away from them and enfold her in my arms. I say to the owl-baby: "Oh, my dear, my little dear, I'm here, I'm finally here, and I'm so sorry I'm late." I take her right out of there and slam the door. Outside is a war zone. B-17 bombardiers are flying overhead, releasing payloads. I hear the rousing "Allegro molto vivace" movement of Tchaikovsky's *Pathétique* Symphony playing out from the sky. The two of us run away together swiftly and triumphantly across the battlefield, where we'll take refuge in an abandoned bunker until it's safe to come out.

"I hate it when you shut down like this," your father is saying. "I hate it when you woolgather. We need to face facts. This Doctor Great will know how to help our little girl."

For your father's benefit, I begin to list all of the great

doctors he has dragged you to see over the years. I remind him of the way each doctor has traumatized you and violated you. I mix in the names of a few more great doctors whom you haven't actually seen, just to see if he is paying attention. Bettelheim. Baumkötter. Mengele.

"Do you think you're very funny?" he says.

His eyes and lips are full of rancor and despair.

"I guess you think you're very funny," he says.

He leaves it alone for a week, and then he comes right back to it. I don't think he means to be unkind. It's just that he thinks he's right, and that I'm the opposite of right, especially when it comes to raising an owl-baby like you. To your father I'm a box that needs to be opened on his way to helping you, and it doesn't really matter to him if he finds the key to me, or if he needs to smash me open with a hammer.

"What's the matter with you, anyway?" he says. "Don't you believe in science?"

"I love my child," I say. "Do you?"

"You think that you and only you can take care of our girl," he says. "Is it some kind of cultural thing? Some kind of overbearing-mother thing? You nearly killed her, you know, the day she was born. The way you ripped her right out of that incubator. My mother was there. She told me she was afraid for you both. She was afraid you'd kill our girl and then they'd arrest you for manslaughter."

Once again, your father has found just the right-sized drill bit to drill into my head and empty it of my convictions.

"Okay, how about this," he says. "Let's try one more doctor. Just one more doctor. Sign here and we can try. Let's take her to see this new doctor in Malibu. I have a great feeling. I've read the research. If this great doctor can't help Charlotte, then we can take a break. I promise. We'll do it your way if it doesn't work this time. Just this once, honey. Please."

He looks at me reasonably. I never understand why he always gets to be the reasonable one in our arguments.

He shifts tactics.

"When I think of what you did at the hospital, the day she was born," he says. "The way you ripped her right out of her incubator. As if you wanted her to die."

I don't answer.

"You wanted our girl to die, didn't you?" he says. "And now you'd rather see her suffer than to give her hope, and a better life. It's some kind of power thing. Some kind of mother thing. Maybe I should have taken away your parental rights long ago."

His shameless historical revisionism takes my breath away.

I wish I had a little grape knife.

I would bury it in his ear.

"I'm sorry," he says. "I'm sorry. I'm just so frustrated. It's horrible to watch her struggle. I can't understand the way you give up on your own child. Can you try to not give up on her? Can't you even try to imagine our girl getting better? Can't you do that, honey? For our girl?"

He is weeping.

"I can't do this by myself any longer," he says. "Our girl deserves better. What's the matter with you, anyway?"

He keeps on threatening and cajoling and fighting and

weeping until I have no bones, not a single bone, and I drip onto the floor in a helpless ooze of guilt and despair.

"All right," I say. "We'll take her. Let's take the owl-baby to see fucking Doctor Great."

"You know I don't like it when you call Charlotte an owl-baby," he says. "It's as if you think she isn't fully human. It's as if you think she's subhuman, just because she has challenges."

I let it go.

Six

On the day of your appointment to see the great Doctor Great, your father straps you into your adaptive car seat at three in the morning and off we go. We're driving from Sacramento to Malibu, instead of taking a flight, because if you tantrum in a plane, then they will land the plane and kick us off and leave us stranded somewhere with nothing but a landing strip surrounded by cornfields. It's a six-hour drive, if we're lucky with the traffic. Your appointment is at nine. You sleep the whole way, a blessing, but as soon as your father pulls into the parking lot of our destination and cuts the engine, your eyes pop open, and you begin to scream in your familiar way. "Hey, honey, come on, Charlotte, stop now, stop, okay-okay, stop, now stop," your father says. He tries to extract you from the car, but you don't want to go with him. The two of you begin your grim familiar battle. The people driving by on a nearby boulevard hear you shrieking. They see a big man trying to subdue a child, and it disturbs them. They honk their horns at us.

"What are you doing to that kid?" they yell out their windows as they pass. "Leave that kid alone, you sickos!"

You never yield, owl-baby, but your father is stronger. After some mild hand-to-hand combat your father has succeeded in rolling you up tight in the blanket he brought along for the purpose of rendering you helpless. He wraps you so tight that you may as well be in a full-body cast. Only your face peeks out, so you can breathe, which means that you can scream. You scream and scream, but there is nothing you can do. Your father carries you over his shoulder in the same way he might carry any rolled-up blanket with a screaming child inside. The lobby is full of banana plants. The great doctor's office is on the eleventh floor. We take the elevator, and every time the doors open on a random floor the people decide to wait for the next elevator to come. The great doctor's waiting area is full of children sitting quietly in their mothers' laps. The children have identical cloth caps on their heads. When one of the children absently pulls on her cap, I see the flash of bright steel, because there is a metal skullcap attached to her brainpan that's as bright and shiny as a chrome bread box.

I can't stop looking.

Her mother sees me looking, and she pulls the cloth cap back over her child's head.

"Oh, thank you, Mother," the child says to her mother. "Thank you for helping me. Having a mother like you is the best thing that ever happened to me, oh, yes, a big thank-you to my mother."

"Listen to that kid, honey," your father says. "Look at what we have to look forward to. A calm kid. A happy kid."

We skip to the front of the line because our child is the disruptive one. A nurse leads us into an examination room that is remarkable for a giant container stuck to the wall that is marked *BIOHAZARD*. You wrench an arm loose from your blanket and rip the container from the wall, and a rain of contaminated needles falls and scatters across the floor. We get out of that room quickly, before you escape from your blanket altogether and start playing with the dirty sharps. Once back in the hallway we see a man who can only be the great doctor himself, emerging from another door. With a take-charge attitude common to those in his profession, he tells us to leave the premises because our screaming child is upsetting his patients. "What about our consultation?" your father says. "We have come all the way from Sacramento this morning. You're our last hope, Doctor Great." The great doctor's face softens unappealingly. With a vapid gesture of his hand he hustles us into another room where there are many diplomas on the wall, plus a glass bowl full of lollipops. You keep sniffing the air, Chouette, which leads me to perceive that the great doctor is wearing Old Spice, and that your diaper needs changing. The great doctor snaps on some gloves. He gestures for your father to deposit you on the steel table. I may be crying. After your father extracts you from your rolled-up blanket, you get away from him completely and you vomit on the great doctor's shoes.

The great doctor gazes down upon you as if he were gazing at a shadow on the wall of a cave.

"We can make tremendous progress with your son, little mother," the great doctor says. "You will see. The results even after the first treatment can be quite miraculous. Even after just one treatment your son will be able to sit quietly and to comply with basic instructions."

"She's a daughter," I say. "Her name is Chouette."

You peck at the great doctor's leg until he covers his privates discreetly, with both hands.

"Dad, help me please to get your child up on the examination table, *houp-là*," the doctor says.

It takes two grown men to hold you down. I don't help because I'm rooting for you. I want you to bruise and bite. I want you to fight and win. But at last the great doctor manages to pin down your splayed little legs, and your father manages to pin down your splayed brittle arms.

A nurse comes in, carrying a giant syringe in both hands.

"What's in that syringe?" I say.

"Not to worry, little mother," the great doctor says. "It's mostly water."

"Water and what else?"

"Mostly water. A bit of vitamin D. A bit of this and that. A very small bit of *benzisoxazole derivative* and *pyrazolyl-alkylpiperazine derivative*. Oh, ho-ho, you can see how difficult these chemical compositions are to pronounce. Never mind. Just a small chemical. Never you mind, small mother. It's FDA-approved. Not to worry. It prepares the brain for the next stage."

"The next stage?"

"Surely you have read about my procedure, little mother."

"It's FDA-approved," your father says. "Come on, honey. This man is the leading world expert in *artificial intelligence*."

"Please, we in the field prefer the term *synthetic intelligence*," the doctor says. "There is nothing artificial about it. But you are correct. After a small procedure your child will have a brain that functions much like any other child's brain."

I begin to understand my role in this scene.

"Hand her over, you monsters!" I shout.

I wrestle you away.

I take you right out of there and slam the door.

You stopped growing a long while ago, at twenty-six inches, and you weigh less than expected because your bones are hollow, but you've always been a challenge to carry because you don't like to hold on unless we're hunting together. By day, your balance is all off. By day, carrying you is like carrying a pile of slippery logs. But this time you know the stakes. You know we need to get out of here. It's a matter of life and death, owl-baby. You braid your long stick-fingers through my hair and you let me take you all the way back to the car without complaint, because you feel what I feel, that we're escaping from a war zone.

Fortunately, there are no bombardiers outside.

Now we're sitting together in the car. I'd drive away with you if I could, but your father has the keys. The sun beats down through the closed windows until we are purified by the sweltering heat. I look out the front windshield until mine eyes fasten on a pair of palm trees, planted in big pots at the edge of the parking lot, and when I lift mine eyes beyond the potted palms, I can just make out the rough, dark expanse of our future together, rising up broodingly in the distance.

Your father's torso appears in the scene.

He gets in the car and slams the door.

"I'm so embarrassed," he says. "I've never been so embarrassed in my life. We need to pay the consultation fee, thank you very much. Eleven hundred bucks. We come all this way and we pay eleven hundred bucks and what for. I should have left you out of it. I should have known you would sabotage it. I guess I can't count on you. I guess I'm alone in this."

Your father turns the ignition and spins out.

"You're a monster," he says.

We drive for about an hour, and the only sound in the car is my child's soft sad wheezes from the back seat. Thankfully she's fallen asleep again, too overwhelmed by the visit with Doctor Great to do otherwise.

I can feel my husband's anger pulsing toward me, in time with the vein in his right temple.

"I'm so done," he says. "I'm so tired. I'm so fed up. After all I've done."

He keeps saying it. It's like a little prayer he keeps repeating. He isn't really talking to me. He's having a deeply private conversation with himself as he drives along. His upper lip curls at some thought or another, and he laughs to himself.

A few minutes later he decides to let me into his conversation, after all.

"Why the hell don't you play the cello anymore?" he says, out of the blue, and then he slams his fist on the wheel for emphasis.

"Not so loud. You'll wake Chouette," I say.

He's breathing in that special way that makes his nostrils flare.

"You give up on everything, don't you?" he says. "Isn't it just like you, to give up on your music, too? The way you gave up on me? The way you gave up on our girl?"

I could tell him that my cello lies in broken pieces behind the locked door of my home studio, and that wharf rats have stolen away the strings, and that my fingers are like sticks, and my arms are weak with pits and scars. I could tell him that my thoughts are out of tune, and that the idea of music feels like an old forgotten memory in a drawer because my girl takes up every breath and every moment of my life.

But I know he's asking me a different question altogether. He doesn't care about my music. He never has. He stopped coming to concerts once we married, as if attending them to begin with was always just part of a courtship ritual that was no longer required of him. He's angry at me for some other reason.

"I don't understand you at all!" he says. "Why don't you have any friends? Why don't you have interests? Why are you so dull and tired all the time?"

Does he really not know what it means to be the mother of an owl-baby?

"What's the matter with you, anyway, Tiny?" he says plaintively.

"I don't know," I say.

It feels too big to say more.

"You don't *know*," he says bitterly.

In such a few words, in just three words, he's managed to tell me how unhappy I make him, and how revolted he is when he looks at me, and how angry he is that I gave him an owl-baby instead of a child who could tie her own shoes, or play catch in the yard, or hug him back, or tell him how much she loves her dad.

And now he's done talking to me. Maybe for good.

We drive along silently until we're home again.

I get out of the car. I help you out of your adaptive car seat. You poor thing. You're bedraggled and pathetic after such a terrible day. Unlike our disagreement after the *tough love* therapy, though, you don't blame me for this latest debacle. You know I'm the one who rescued you in your darkest hour. You grace me with a little "ca-caw," a sound that I think may mean: "Thank you, Mom." Your father strides off angrily, not helping, because he needs his time to sulk in his room above the garage. And it's so strange, owl-baby. Instead of beating my spirit down, the way your father's words and deeds might have done on any other day, his pettiness and his outbursts and his self-serving harangues of the day have clarified things for me. I finally see how wrong he is about you. How wrong he is about everything. All your father knows is how to crush your spirit. All your father wants is to make you into a grotesque imitation of a dog-child. And all of the doubts that your father has poured into my ear, across the years, flow out of me, and my mother-instinct flows back into my veins like a fast transfusion.

I am your champion.

I am your mother.

Tonight our hunt will be gorgeous and vivid. It will be bloody and perfect. We will rip and tear and feast.

"Acka-tac-tac!" you shout.

We exult in our plan.

After it's completely dark, we leave softly together through a little window. The sky is moonless and our pupils dilate. I carry you on my back, and you open your webbed arms and stretch your pencil-fingers wide, as if to carry us both aloft. There is the smell of blood in the air that reminds me of my childhood in the gloaming, when I hunted rabbits with my little bow. We run through the crisp night air until the memory of the awful Malibu-day blows off of our skins, and we're free again. When we come to the end of the paved roads, you huff and laugh, and when we get to the first line of trees—birches, luminous even in this dark—you give your first real hoot of the night.

"Go on, Chouette," I say. "Wherever you lead me, I'll follow."

You shriek ecstatically, just once, and bound away into the dark, bounding away—nearly flying—while I do my sorry best to keep up. When did you become so strong and swift? When did you learn to bound along so effortlessly—nearly aloft—sometimes rising up nearly as high as the trees? I lose sight of you. I'm running through bramble. I'm running on instinct. Hours pass. The moon rises and sets. I'm lost until I see the orange-haze glow to the east: not the dawn but lights from the highway. The lights orient me. I follow the streamed and splash upstream through shallow waters, straining to see you ahead. I hear dogs barking in the distance, or maybe it's sirens. I slip and fall in the muck. I climb up the embankment, through sticks and trees and weeds, and I begin to walk along the ridge, searching for a glimpse of you. To the left I see the harsh, glorious tangle of the wild thicket. To the right I see a rigid pattern of tended fields, long lines of crops dug into the earth. I see everything. I'm exhilarated. I'm imagining you on your great adventure. I feel like howling at the stars.

But then I hear the most terrible scream.

I hear it in my breasts, and skin, and heart.

It's like no sound I've ever heard, and yet I know it's my precious girl.

And I come running, dirt sliding, leaves sparkling, until I burst into an open place—where I see you, suspended and splayed, as if in midair. At first I don't understand. And then I see the web: You're caught in a net, set there to keep birds from the crops. Dozens of little birds are hanging dead in the net all around you. You're in a panic, trying to wrench free. Your struggles are making these hanged dead birds shake and dance grotesquely. You've stirred up the flies. The fine nylon netting digs into you, garroting your limbs. You're so afraid. I try to soothe. I try to untangle. There, there, Chouette. You wrench away from me, fighting me. You entangle yourself deeper. We start over. I try again to soothe. I try to unhook you. I try to calm you. It goes easier this time because you've exhausted yourself. When you feel the first arm come free of the net, you strike out blindly, because you're terrified. Tenderly, tenderly—I soothe you. I cherish you.

I hold you to my breast like a babe until you see me.

It's Mother, Chouette.

You see me now. You're calming down.

You're calm.

You let me help you. We're almost done.

And then you're free.

I don't think you're hurt too badly, but you're trembling.

I soothe and stroke.

"I love you, Chouette. You're all right now."

Together we make our slow way home. It's almost light. We're very late. Your father is backing his car out of the driveway. He's on his way to work. When he sees us, he jumps out of the car. Already he has his phone in his hand. He's calling 9-1-1 so the gendarmes can come get me. He will never understand. I'm shaking. I'm lost. He's found us out. He's running toward us.

"Chouette got out of the house somehow," I say. "I was afraid. I ran after her."

All of these are true statements, however empty they are of the full truth.

I brace myself for his interrogations.

"Tiny, you're very badly hurt!" he says.

His voice is an anguished garble, and he looks frightened.

"I'm all right," I say. "It's Chouette we need to worry about. She's been shaken up."

He takes you away from me. He isn't looking at you at all. He's looking at me. He's at a loss. You're fine, actually. You're safe and unhurt. I'm the one who is all sticky and red. I'm so relieved that I sit right down on the sidewalk. Your father sits next to me. He's ripped off his starched-white shirt and he's pressing the cloth against my face, to stanch the flow.

You look on blandly until the ambulance comes for me.

To tell the truth, in these last few weeks I've been feeling knocked down by recent events. I'm taking antibiotics and painkillers. My face itches. I lie on this little sofa for hours and days. When I look in the mirror, I can tell that I'm going to be left with a fashionable dueling scar from our last night in the woods together. Your father has taken a leave of absence from work to care for us. He's calling doctors on my behalf. I barely get to see you these days. I feel an ominous, gathering cloud, pressing in from all sides. I'm afraid for you. I'm afraid for me. Our lovely life, so full of nocturnal ecstasies, is crumbling at the edges. Nothing perfect ever lasts. I know that from experience. My daytime slumbers grow deeper, from the painkillers, and my thoughts darker, and my disorientation more complete, until here, now, as I lie here on this little sofa, just barely on the way to being awake, my first thought when I open my eyes and see you is: Didn't I dress you in your pink jumpsuit today? So why are you wearing that floral party dress now?

Your father is there to explain my worries away.

"Oh, don't worry about the pink jumpsuit, honey. Charlotte had a little accident while you were sleeping. That's all. The jumpsuit's in the laundry—hey, look, I've fixed us supper tonight."

Your father never cooks. He's up to something.

"I'm not hungry," I say.

The doctors say I'm on the mend. I'm feeling pressed on all sides, though, by an ever-present suspicion that your father is continuing his search for a way to fix you, all the more so now that I've been temporarily sidelined. Also, I'm not sure if he's feeding you fresh meats. I'm worried that a sudden change of diet won't agree with you. I imagine he's taking advantage of the way I've been knocked down by life. For a few days more, at least, as my wounds heal, I can't be as diligent in looking after you as I would like to be. Your father never gives up on anything, especially not when he is wrong. I imagine him taking you back to see Doctor Great on his own. I imagine him bribing many other doctors into accepting you for their dangerously experimental trials. He is probably feeding you illegal drugs and homeopathic doses of fecal matter and other untried medical fixes and not even telling me about it.

When I insist that he tell me the truth, he soothes me.

"Of course not," he says. "I would never. We're a team. That's just mindless paranoia on your part. Settle down. Rest. You're still not at full strength, honey. You're not thinking straight." Yabber-yabber.

My afternoon naps are growing longer at both ends, and I wake up more tired than before. It's a stress-induced, mild form of narcolepsy. Or maybe your father is drugging me. Maybe he is adding some special *this and that* to my prescriptions.

A little *this* to keep me placid. A little *that* to keep me out of his way. A bit of phenobarbital. A pinch of diazepam. A dusting of strychnine from the box I keep under the sink to keep the rat population down. Or maybe your father is right when he tells me that it's just my mindless paranoia talking. That seems more likely, doesn't it, owl-baby?

Sometimes when I listen to my tangled thoughts, I think your father must be right.

Sometimes when I wake up, I think that you smell clinical, and I wonder if your father has taken you somewhere without telling me.

Sometimes your father's face will be newly wounded, as if he has been scratched by you in a scuffle; or there will be sticky, glue-ish stuff in your hair, as if you have just come back from a brain scan where they attached electrodes to your head, and your father didn't have time to clean you up correctly before I opened my eyes.

I don't trust your father.

After you begin to exhibit new spurts of precocity, I think my suspicions must be true, and that your father has been taking you behind my back to some brand-new therapy or another, and that he's taking advantage of my temporary health setback to try to squeeze in a few more fixes, before I'm fully recovered.

You're not able to say a word, and maybe you will never say a word, but one day you know the letters of the alphabet.

"Where is the *O*?" your father will say, and you take your little wet claw out of your mouth and point to the *O* in your little cloth alphabet book. "Where is the *B*? Where is the *T*?" he says. You are right every time.

And then, another astonishment, a few weeks after you learn to point out the letters of the alphabet, you learn to write. Unbelievable. You haven't spoken a word outside of "caw" or "hss," and yet here you are writing your letters. All day long you scrabble around the house writing on the floor with a fat piece of playground chalk. The smooth wooden planks in the dining room are your preferred writing surface. You write vertically, in columns. Your writing appears to be nonsense strings of meaningless symbols, but I can't be sure. You write your capital *A*'s upside down so they look like an Egyptian hieroglyph of a cow's head. Your father copies down your letters in a notebook. Why am I so afraid? Why do these new astonishments from you seem unnatural when I've seen and accepted the miracle of you bringing down prey with a single, perfect death-stroke of your beak?

I decide it's wrong for me to be nervous about these new developments simply because your father is excited about them.

I remind myself of the many ways I've underestimated you, through the years, since the day I became your mother.

As your father says: "When it comes to our little girl, *can't* is a dirty word."

I know I'm asleep, but I can't wake myself up. I'm feeling as pressed and as helpless as if I were trapped under a wooden plank. The dog-villagers are taking turns placing stones down on the plank, one by one, pressing me flat. Their plan is to keep adding their stones until the stones crush me and I die. At the last minute I find a way to wrench my eyes open, and I see you sitting across the room from me, straight-backed and uncharacteristically quiet in your father's lap. You have a little cloth cap on your head and you're staring at me. You never stare at me. You never sit in your father's lap. You never sit. You look like a ventriloquist's dummy. Your body looks as if it's made of wood. Is it a dream? Am I asleep? Am I a victim of *night-paralysis*? I'm terribly disturbed by the way you are perching straight-backed on your father's knee. I look at you, looking at me. It's like peering into an empty box.

I sit up.

"You've hurt the owl-baby somehow," I say.

"Don't be stupid. I would never hurt our girl."

He's lying about something.

"What have you done to Chouette?" I say.

"It's what we talked about. Doctor Great's procedure," he says.

"Doctor Great's procedure?"

"The procedure. The small procedure. He's given Charlotte *synthetic intelligence*. It helps the brain sort itself out. You know this. You signed the papers. We've talked it over for days and years and forever. We were lucky to get Charlotte into this year's trial. We talked about it, honey. Doctor Great was worried Charlotte might be getting too old, but the brain scans gave him hope that it was not too late. The younger the child, the better the results, he says. We'll have to see, won't we? Yabber-yabber. Anyway, it's done."

I don't scream or shout. I make a sound like this: "Ah, ah, ah."

"Don't act so surprised," he says. "Next we can work on her appearance. I've been in touch with a cosmetic surgeon who thinks there's a fine chance of fashioning a proper nose for our Charlotte. We only need to shave off a bit of her femur, to make the nose-bridge."

Every time I inhale, I sound like a dying bull taking its last breath.

Every time I exhale it sounds like I'm already dead.

"You can't argue with results," your father says. "Oh, honey, settle down, don't scare her with your antics, we talked about this. We talked and talked about it. I know you don't always remember everything about the *day-to-day*. I know you're more of a *big-picture* kind of gal. You're the dreamer in our family. It's why I love you. It's you and me, together. We did this for our girl. We finally did it."

"I signed the papers?"

"Why wouldn't you sign the papers? We both want what's best for our girl."

My husband's eyes are full of hope and love.

Your eyes look as if they're made of cheap glass. Your scalp is half shaved. A long electric cord wraps around your ear and then disappears inside your head. The top of your head is covered with a metal skullcap, as bright and shiny as a chrome bread box.

"Chouette?" I whisper.

"Hello, Mother," you say.

I close my eyes. I open them. Everything is the same. Has he lobotomized you? You look lobotomized. I can't see your inner spirit. I listen dully as your father explains how two holes have been drilled in your skull—two infinitely small, barely-there holes, he says—and through these holes the great Doctor Great has inserted a box crammed full of *synthetic intelligence*, and covered your head back over with a nice chrome lid so he can get back in there whenever you need an upgrade.

"It's FDA-approved," your father says.

I can barely hear your father's yabber-yabber because the bats and bandicoots are shrieking just outside the doors, and the rabbits are screaming in the attic, and the wood shrews are rustling in their nests. I hear their death-howls and wild protestations. I'm cold. I'm made of ice. My fingers are blue because the blood is drawing close to my heart.

"Nothing dangerous, nothing untested," your father says. "Nothing but a *language-approximation device*. Please, honey, please. We're all born with the skills we need, each and every one of us. Except for some of us who are born without the skills we need. Don't get upset. If we didn't give our girl this chance, it would be like we were child abusers. It would be like withholding insulin from a diabetic. It would be like withholding water from an overheated dog. It's done. She's fixed."

"Chouette?" I say. "Honey?"

"Nobody home," you say.

"My God, will you listen to her talk," your father says.

"Take that box out of her head," I say. "Take it out right now."

"Isn't that just like you, to piss on a miracle," he says. "By the end of the year our girl will be speaking like a normal kid."

I'm paralyzed. I can't think straight.

Your father carries you over to me and puts you in my lap.

"She's still our sweet little girl," he says. "Please, honey. We talked and talked about it. I heard your side. Then you heard my side. I'm on the right side. We're in this together. Look at our girl, sweetheart. Listen to her speak."

"My mother is so supportive," you say. "Having a mother who is always there for you is the best thing that can happen to a child. Yes, a big thank-you to my mother."

"There, you see?" your father says. "We need to practice with her every day. We're supposed to ask the questions on this list until she gets the idea."

He tries to hand me his preprinted list of questions.

I slap his hand away.

"'Question One,'" your father says, unperturbed. "'What is your name, little girl?'"

He pronounces each word distinctly.

"I'm not a girl," you say. "I'm an American Owl-Baby."

"You are a girl."

"I'm an American Owl-Baby!"

"Leave her alone," I say.

"You are a girl," your father says.

"You are a girl," you say.

"No," your father says patiently. "I am a man, and I am your father. You are a girl. Your name is Charlotte. 'Question One: What is your *name*, little girl?'"

You close your eyes tightly and you shriek in your familiar way, and my heart soars.

"Look, Tiny, you can help her, I know you can," your father says to me. "You're her mother. After you get her calmed down, why don't you take a crack at these questions? Come on, don't upset her. I can't believe you're not thrilled. I know it's a shock. It's a miracle, that's what it is. Come on. She's spent more time with you than she has with me. She's accustomed to your speech patterns. Show me how to do it."

He tries to hand me his goddamn list of questions again.

"Come on, just try, ask her a question," your father says. "Take the list. Try Question Two."

"No," I say.

"Take it, take it," he says.

I grab his list out of his hands and crumple it and throw it down.

He grabs it up again and smooths it out.

"'Question Two: What do you think of your mother?'" he says.

"My mother is so supportive," you say. "Having a mother who is always there for you is the best thing that can happen to a child. Yes, a big thank-you to my mother."

You suck on your little claw, just like the day you were born.

"Good girl!" your father says.

When your attention wanders, he claps his hands.

"Charlotte! Listen up! Over here, girl! Here, girl! Look at me!" he says. "'Question Three: What do you think of your father?'"

"My father is really handsome. My father is the kindest, bravest, warmest, most wonderful human being I've ever known in my life."

"My God," he says. "Did you ever think we'd see the day, honey? Now, give us a smile, Charlotte, hey-ho, over here! Look this way! Charlotte! Give us a smile!"

"Smiley, Shiley!" you shriek.

"Smile, Charlotte!" your father says. "Show your mother how happy you are!"

"Good-bye!" you say.

"Are you all right, Chouette?" I say.

You close your eyes and blow a raspberry.

"Jesus, you messed it up already," your father says. "You asked a question that isn't on the list. Look how she shut down. You're supposed to stick to the questions on the list."

He picks you up from my lap.

"Thank you, Dad!" you shout.

"Good girl!" your father says.

You cough up a pellet on his starched-white shirt, and then you strain for me, reaching out, until your father hands you back over. You find all of my familiar soft spaces, and then you begin to cry, in a shrill, doggish way that I've never heard before. Oh, dear one, what have they done to you? How could I have allowed it? Something now is tick-tock-ticking in your brain, erasing your owl-thoughts and overwriting them with dog-thoughts.

But I won't surrender you to them, Chouette. Tonight, after your father goes to sleep, I'll ask you all the important questions, and then we'll go out in the night together, and we'll avoid any nets or man-made impediments, and you'll remember who you are.

After your father goes to sleep that night, I come softly to your room to wake you. I'm feeling weak but determined. Raw meat will lift our spirits. Fresh blood will shake you from your dog-stupor.

"Chouette," I whisper. "Get up. It's dark. It's time to go."

You stretch and sigh.

"Oh, Mother," you say.

I'm startled to hear the dog-language coming from your throat.

"I can't go anywhere with *you*, you silly," you say.

"Why not? Let's go!"

"My father says to stay right here."

"Your father is asleep."

"I'm asleep, too," you say.

You shut your eyes, and you won't open them again, and

when I try to pick you up, you peck at my hand, a warning, and that's the end of it.

The next night I try again.

"What about now, Chouette? Shouldn't we go out tonight, dear, in the dark?"

"Oh, Mother. I'm exactly where I need to be."

"Are you happy, honey?"

"Well, you could say I'm so, so happy," you say.

"Let's go out, then," I say.

"My mother is so supportive. Having a mother who is always there for you is the best thing that can happen to a child. Yes, a big thank-you to my mother."

I reach out with my bandaged hand. You don't attack it. I try to pick you up and you allow it. You let me hold you and hug you until I'm crying. I've missed you so much.

"Are you ready? Let's go. It's dark. Your father is asleep."

"No. You're bad. You're bad for me."

"Please. Your father is asleep. He isn't going to miss you."

"Miss me, yourself."

"You're scaring me, Chouette."

"A big thank-you to my mother."

"I *love* you, Chouette."

"Crush and rip," you say. "Chirrup. My mother is so supportive. My father is really handsome. When are you going to let me rip off your head?"

On the third night when I wake you and ask you once again to come out with me into the night, you say: "Where?" And even though I'm still startled at the dog-speak coming out of your chitinous lips, I feel a stab of hope.

"Let's go and see. We can go wherever you like, and come back when you like."

"What does Dad say?"

"He's not going to know."

You consider it.

"Okay," you say.

We slip out together. We go to your former-favorite hunting spot, out beyond the line of birches, where the housing developments still haven't swallowed the wild world. I'll keep you far from the deadly net tonight, my dear.

You won't leave my arms. You're as helpless as a newborn.

You can't remember how to catch and kill, or how to wait in silence for your prey to reveal itself.

"Oopsy-daisy!" you say. "That's all right! Oh, that's a ball! That's a cup! That's a doll! Yeah! Time to clean up! Clean up everywhere! Oopsy-daisy, don't drop the spoons! You wouldn't hurt a fly! You never would! You're good! You're all right!"

You look at me with terror in your eyes.

Women of the world: Do you know the feeling of seeing your child in terror and not being able to save her?

Do you know that most terrible feeling?

Are you a mother, too?

There is no owl-baby left in you. Doctor Great has won. Your father has won. You can mimic all the ways of a perfect dog-child. Your old pleasures no longer interest you. You no longer revel in eating live food; you prefer it puréed. You can use a spoon and never drop it. You've learned table manners. You're soft and gentle and you never lash out at anyone. When your grandmother calls, your father hands you the phone so you can chat with her. "Where are you, Grammy?" you say in your sweet little dog-voice, and I can hear her smoker's-baritone reply: "Why, hunny-bunny, I'm right here in my snug little house! When are you coming over for a visit with your grammy?" And you reply: "Oh! A visit to my grammy's house will make me so, so happy!" Day by day I feel you slipping away from me. I can't wake you at night. You mumble in your sleep and roll over.

I try to keep our daytime routine the same as before, at least. I take you to our favorite park down the road so that you can climb on the play structures, just the way you've loved to do for many years. But when we get to the park, instead of whooping and shrieking and climbing, and instead of making playful stabbing gestures with your talon toward the other children, you say to me in matter-of-fact dog-words, "I'm bored, Mother. I see nothing of interest here. Why do we always do the same things, over and over again? Why do you keep me from doing the things I love?"

"I don't keep you from doing the things you love," I say.

"You're wrong about that. You love coming here to the park with me. You love climbing higher than any other child can climb. You love looking down from your high perch and hooting out your feelings while I wait below."

"I don't love those things. It's you who love those things, Mother."

"You love them, too, Chouette. You've always loved them."

"I love you, Mother," you say. "You are the one I love. My mother is so supportive. My father is really handsome. The weather is very fine today."

I'm thinking I may take you back to church with me. It's pathetic to turn to religion in my darkest hour, but that's the way it is. I second-guess the decision I made, long ago, to never go back there. I even begin to imagine that a church community may teach you how to *honor thy mother*, which is something you've forgotten lately, little missy.

"I'm going to church this Sunday and you're going with me," I say.

"I don't want to go. I hate that place, and I hate you," you say.

You sound so much like a normal dog-child that your father looks up in delight.

"Hey, kid, no backtalk," he says. "Children need to listen to their parents."

The following Sunday, off we go to church. I don't really want to go. I just want to win an argument for a change. Your father is happy to drive us that morning because you keep saying: "I love you, Dad." He's aglow with father-joy. As for me, I'm pondering the uses of my life as we drive along. I'm wondering whether each word and thought, from the time our mothers first birth us out into this world, is prompted by a *language-approximation device* that most of us happen to be born with, and whether this impression we have, that we think original thoughts, is nothing but a happy illusion. I wonder if we are born programmed to behave as we do, and to say what we say. Maybe it's true, what your father believes, that *synthetic intelligence* is exactly the fix you needed. You keep chattering away in my lap: "There's a cow. I love bananas! Dum dum brrr." You don't love bananas. Bananas repulse you. Is life nothing more than a continuous retreat from our own true selves, as we're hammered into shape by special schools and social cues? Can I trust this thought I'm thinking now? Is it my thought? I begin to breathe very quickly. I calm myself by humming the second movement of Brahms's *Ein Deutsches Requiem*, the part where the chorus declares *"Denn alles Fleisch, es ist wie Gras."* My breathing slows and deepens with the swell of music in my head, and I recover my equilibrium.

Your father pulls up to the curb and waits for us to get out, and then he drives away.

Maybe the church ladies will remember the time you tried to peck out the eye of a woman in the blue suit, long ago, and will throw stones at us. Or maybe I'm wrong about that entire episode. Maybe, after prayerful reflection, the woman in the blue suit decided to forgive, just as Jesus taught her to forgive.

Maybe she has been waiting for us all this time to come back to church so she can tell us herself that she's forgiven our trespasses.

I don't see the woman in the blue suit anywhere. I'm disappointed to have expended so much thought in her direction needlessly.

An anonymous greeter comes forward.

"Welcome, welcome," he says.

"I love my father," you say. "My father is very handsome."

"What a delightful little girl you have there," the greeter says. "She loves her dad."

He leads us into the church through the tall oak doors and he seats us in front. You're still the most special child here by a long shot, and the window behind the altar still depicts a standard contemporary rendering of a risen Christ with a little dove in his hand. The enormous and deep baptismal font in front of the altar is exactly the same as before—big enough and deep enough to submerge a grown person. One could drown in that baptismal font. The people file in. The organ sounds. The choir begins to sing. The same pastor emerges from his secret door. Yabber-yabber. There is call and response. There is weeping and gnashing of teeth. "Take me and eat me," the pastor says, and my heart leaps when I feel you strain toward him in response to those carnal yet familiar words. You betray yourself, owl-baby. In spite of your father's muckery inside your head, your killer instinct remains.

The time comes for me to bring you forward to the altar and to offer you up for a blessing.

The pastor anoints you with oil.

He pauses.

Something different happens.

The pastor leans forward and peers into your eyes.

"The child is not herself," the pastor shouts magisterially. "Something is blocking this child's spirit. Something *evil*."

He turns to his congregation. His voice booms out.

"Pray, my sisters and brothers, for the truth to be revealed! Pray that this child's spirit be restored unto her! The devil has taken hold in her!"

You lie there in his arms. You're looking up at him in wonder.

"There is something *hard* and *foreign* in this child! I can feel it in her *soul*!" the pastor shouts.

"It's in her head," I say.

"Out, Devil, out!" he says.

"Out, Devil!" the people shout.

I feel faith sprouting up in me like green living things, and I shout with the rest of them: "Out, Devil, out!" Without warning the pastor plunges you into the waters of the baptismal font—oh, is that really best? is that really necessary?—and he holds you down there for a few seconds, and after that he holds you down there a few more seconds. I try to rescue you from drowning, but the pastor holds me off with one straight arm. To tell the truth, you aren't even struggling under there. You look happy. I let go of my doubts. I pray and shout with the rest of them because I want the devil out of you as much as they do. I want you to be the child you were when you needed me. I want to believe.

The pastor lifts you up from the waters.

For a few seconds I recognize you. For a few seconds

you're almost completely back to your old self. I can see it in your eyes, owl-baby. It's a miracle. It's you. You're yourself again. You're my fate and you're my dire necessity. You're my refuge when I'm lost, and losing you would kill me. Your flights and falls are dreamlike and perfect and I'm blessed to be the one to witness them.

Your eyes go dead.

You begin to cry in your new, dog-child way.

I've lost you again.

"There, there," the pastor says. "I hear you, little one."

He pats your back until you spit up on his shoulder.

"Let us pray," he says, and the service moves on.

I'm very disappointed.

When your father comes to collect us, you're wet and you smell like vomit, and he says: "Good Lord, what did you let these fuckers do to her!" He gathers you into his arms and you don't resist.

"I love you, Charlotte," he whispers into your small tufted ear. "You're safe now, sweetheart. I'll be taking care of you from now on."

As well you know, owl-baby, ever since you were born, and every year since, your father has never once taken you along to a single Annual Summer Barbecue, or even to a Thanksgiving Feast, even though every year I've pleaded with him to accept you as a member of his own family, and to champion you, and to love you as his own beloved child at these gatherings. I've hated forever the way your father would insist each year on going by himself, leaving us behind like cast-offs—as if you were a mistaken, corrupt thing instead of our beautiful child.

But now that you have *synthetic intelligence*, his feeling about you has changed completely. Now he thinks you're ready to join his family. He wants to show you off. Now that you can speak some dog-words, it seems your father can overlook any amount of owlness about you. Now that you can say the words "I love you, Dad!" he thinks that the grandparents and aunts and uncles will accept you, and that your cousins will accept you. Never mind that you'll never grow much beyond the size of a shopping bag. Never mind that you climb and scrabble. Never mind that you still try to peck out your father's eye, now and then. None of that matters to your father, now that you can say: "I love you, Dad!"

I feel myself digging in.

I hear myself say: "You can't take her. I won't let you."

"Come on! Really?" your father says. "You've wanted to take her every year and now you want to stay home?"

"That's right. Why do you want to take her now when you didn't think she was good enough for your family before?"

"What's wrong with you?" your father says. "I mean, what literally the hell is wrong with you? Are you sick in the head? I want to take her because I worry about leaving her alone with you these days! Did you know that? The things you say to her! The things you do to her! Unbelievable! I don't think you've cleaned a dish in a month! I don't think you've cleaned the bathroom in a year! The refrigerator is full of rancid meat! The bathrooms smell like dead rat!"

"Shut up," I say.

"Dead rat!" he says. "I don't care. I'm past caring. Stay home if you want. I'm taking her. Maybe you can clean up while we're gone. Maybe you can take a bath for once. I'll take Charlotte myself."

"You'd like that, wouldn't you?" I say.

"I'm so tired of this argument," your father says. "You're crazy. I'm taking my girl to see my parents. You can come. Or you can stay home. It's up to you."

It's happening right now. Our little family is on our way, right now, to the Annual Summer Barbecue. You'll get to meet all your cousins and aunts and uncles, and they'll have a chance to form their opinions. Now we're driving up the sweeping semicircular driveway to the rambling old farmhouse where your father spent his childhood. Your cousins are splashing in the pool on this midsummer Central Valley day. Your uncles are waiting for your father to arrive so that they can begin their vituperative game of volleyball. My mother-in-law and my father-in-law stand on the porch like alien dignitaries. My mother-in-law's rescue birds are bunched up in the driveway. It's a larger flock than I remember—my mother-in-law has been busy taking in peacocks without tails, and wild turkeys so full of buckshot that they need to drag themselves along the ground as they walk. The birds on the drive part to let our car pass, and then they reassemble to the rear of the car, where they begin to follow us in neat rows. We are a procession of sad broken things. You wrenched yourself free of your latest adaptive car seat along the way, rendering it useless, and now you're asleep in my arms and your diaper is leaking. Your father brings the car to a halt. I get out of the car with you still in my arms. My mother-in-law's rescue birds gather 'round and peck at my bare feet in supplication. My mother-in-law is speaking in a polite and gracious tone from the porch, but her feelings are enormous and they make her tremble. My mother-in-law's smile looks like a bared-teeth appeasement display. Her husband is also smiling, in his case a bit vacantly on account of his semantic dementia. I interpret the old man's smile as a bid for forgiveness, for that time at the hospital, just after you were born, when he tried to rip you from my arms. Your father skips up the wooden porch stairs, and he kisses both parents with exuberant smacks. My mother-in-law begins a conversation with her son about the online research she's been doing lately on the subject of rare congenital defects. Soon she is on a tear about metabolic anomalies and brain disorders caused by agricultural pesticides in drinking water and I haven't even reached the first step of her front porch. Popping up from the inane thicket of my mother-in-law's remarks, I hear an undertone of rabid growls and hostile whispers. Then I realize that what I'm hearing is recorded music, drifting out from inside the house. It's Stravinsky's *Rite of Spring*, not in its typical symphonic production but instead performed on one piano, four hands.

Stravinsky and Debussy used to play this arrangement of *Rite of Spring* on a piano together at private gatherings, playing the loud parts with such gusto that they would break strings. I had sent this recording to my parents-in-law at some point as a goodwill gift. It's likely they are playing it now for the first time, to make me feel welcome. In spite of this peace offering I don't forgive them for their outrageous territorial display at the hospital on the day you were born. I'm not clearheaded enough to care in the slightest about my manners. I have come eleven miles in a car with an excreting owl-baby in my lap, and consequently both I and the owl-baby are befouled and in need of a good scrub, and our limbs are stiff. The rescue birds on the lawn ululate the story of their stunted lives. These days I can't smell a thing around my girl, but I'm alert enough to pick up the signals from my parents-in-law that they are dismayed by the reality of Chouette; that they are possibly having feelings akin to *buyer's remorse* for inviting us to this year's Annual Summer Barbecue. None of the other family members have come out of their safe spaces to meet the owl-baby member in the family. My feet are barefoot, and in spite of my feet being the cleanest thing about me, I know it will disturb my mother-in-law to have me walk into her house without proper foot-coverings and that is why I do it. Your father has been coaching you for weeks to try to get you to say "I love you, Grammy," and "I love you, Grampa." No dice. As the two of us walk past, you don't say a word to either of them. You snub them both. I don't stop. I go right in. It's been years since I've been in this house, and yet it's startlingly the same, in the way of houses owned by geriatrics. Your aunts are sitting around in the living room, drinking and knitting, the way they always do before it's time to make the salads in the kitchen. As soon as they see us, they stop talking. My *former secret lover* is there, too, of course. Seeing her again feels like I've just found an old teacup in a cabinet, and the teacup reminds me of a time in my past when I used to drink tea. She looks at you with terror in her eye and grabs her dull kid closer.

In the evening, after the steaks have been barbecued and eaten, and when almost everyone in the family is busy napping and digesting, a time comes when someone in your father's family is finally kind to you. It's your increasingly demented grandfather, who rarely does more these days than sit and stare at the slippers on his feet. He has asked me if he can hold you, Chouette. Even though his dementia is quite alarming at times, he seems lucid just now. His voice, when he asks to hold you, is calm and sad, as if he's reminding himself of all the snubs his family has subjected him to in these last years, and as if he identifies with you because of them. Even though I don't fully trust his child-holding skills at this stage of his life, no one else has asked to hold you at all. I'm overflowing with gratefulness at his gesture, and in spite of my misgivings I decide to let him. I do that. I feel sorry for him. His wife would rather look away than help him when he dribbles food on his bib. He's well on his way to becoming an owl-baby himself. Now my father-in-law is holding you like an old pro.

He raised six boys of his own, and the body-memory of holding all those boys, those many years ago, helps him remember how to do it now. "Pookadoo, pookadoo," he says, and he's delighted when you say it back to him. He pats your back in a loving manner, and he manages to say to me above your continuous dog-babble: "You worry too much, little mother. There is nothing wrong with your girl. Your girl came into this world exactly as she was meant to be." We're standing together by the tranquil pool that has been the scene for many a happy family gathering in the past. The old boy is literally in tears because, even though his short-term memory is shot, he can still remember those good old times when his boys were youngsters, splashing in this very pool. It's a beautiful spot. It's getting on toward evening. The dog-children have come out of the pool hours ago and now they're inside watching cable cartoons. The water in the pool is still and calm for the first time all day. We're surrounded by the vast green irrigated yard where the sprinklers are shooting out jets of water in a pleasant rhythm. The rescue birds are languidly preening over by the driveway, and now and then they call out, and their calls fill the still air with a plaintive loveliness. Some starlings fly over, swift silhouettes that swirl across the evening sky. Any grudge I might have held toward this old man disappears in that instant as I watch him rub your back. No one in the family has ever told me what my father-in-law has just told me: that we are meant to love you, Chouette, for exactly who you are.

"There is nothing wrong with your little girl," he assures me.

"Thank you, Dad," I say.

I feel a floaty wonder to have discovered such an unlikely ally.

That's when my father-in-law unexpectedly throws you in the deep end of the pool.

You fly to the bottom, headfirst, like a loon. You're the "sinker" part of "hook, line, and sinker." My father-in-law peers down, waiting for you to learn from adversity, the way his six boys once learned from adversity on their way to becoming swimmers after he threw them into the pool in just this way, back in the day when that's what fathers did for their sons. For a moment I stand still-as-a-rock next to him, trying to make sense of the scene. I think back on the long-ago day when you were last in a pool, at the Therapeutic Swim Center, and I mimic the swim coach and leap in after you. I struggle down to the level where you've sunk to and I grab you by one arm. I can't see. My eyes cloud. We break the surface and I don't know how we got there.

I hear my father-in-law shout from the pool deck, "I taught all my boys to swim in this very pool, in this same way, and your girl is no different, she'd learn to be a fine strong swimmer for sure if you didn't spoil her so much, little mother!" before he totters off.

We're alone in the deep end. We're losing, and we're drowning. I didn't take off my shoes before I jumped in, and now my shoes want to drag us both down under. My skirt wraps around my legs like the burial shroud. I'm a poor swimmer. I swallow and spit.

And still, somehow, I drag you toward the shallow end.

I feel the cement bottom of the pool under my feet.

I pull you out.

We lie there on the pool deck like half-dead things after a flood.

You're screaming and choking. That means that you're still breathing, and so I scream along with you while I try to understand what just happened to us. I must have bit my tongue hard at some point because now I taste blood inside my mouth and feel blood gushing out from my lips. Our screams are making the dogs howl. The rest of the family comes running from all directions because they're terrified that one of their own precious little ones has been hurt.

Oh. Just the owl-baby and her crazy mother. They keep their distance. They're frightened of us both. They're frightened by the blood pulsing from my mouth and by the methodical way you keep pecking me, searching for the eyes and other soft parts.

It's then that I realize you're back to your old self, Chouette. Your grandfather threw you into the pool, and you sank to the bottom, and you got dragged out by me, and now you're my old Chouette. Here you are again, my dear owl-baby, striking at my arms and face. You are being exactly yourself, shrieking and shitting and using owl-words. Your trip to the bottom of the pool must have shorted out your *synthetic intelligence*. Right away I think back on the way you became yourself briefly, just after your surprise baptism at the Sunday Service. I'd credited God for that miracle. Now I can see that it was the holy water that did the trick, and that holy water is not even a requirement—that any old water will do. No one comes near. I struggle to stand up, with you in my arms. They're staring at us, owl-baby. Gallons of water stream from our clothes. They're keeping their distance. Is this the moment when I no longer care what your father and his family think of us? Is this the moment I'm ready to abandon all pretense of trying to make these dog-people love you as much as I love you? Your father is striding toward us across the broad lawn with disgust in his eye, but I run away from him and his righteousness; I run away, with you in my arms and my shoes squelching, across the broad lawn and straight toward the gaggle of broken birds that are busy eating worms and grit by a leaking sprinkler.

There we squat, in the muck and grit.

We have found refuge with our kind, with the birds.

When your father catches up, he squats down next to us.

"Why do you always make a goddamn scene?" he hisses. "Why must you always make a goddamn spectacle of yourself?"

He tries to shield us from the looks of his family with his broad back while the rest of his family distributes itself across the lawn in an attempt to find a better view. The teens have their phones out. They're filming the whole wild scene so they can upload it later and amaze their friends. You and I fit right in with these tatty rescue birds, owl-baby. Since squatting here among the birds, you've stopped screaming. You've grown calm.

How beautiful and bold you are, my girl.

"Fucking hell," your father says. "What the fucking hell. What the serious fucking hell. Give me Charlotte. Hand her over."

He makes a grab for you. Good girl: You draw first blood, and then you piss on his trousers. Your father's dog-instincts kick in and he slaps you hard. I grab a fistful of grit and dirt and throw it in his face. I take you up into my arms again, protecting you. I rock and soothe. "Christ," your father says. He is squinting because his eyes are full of grit. The rescue birds are silent witnesses, monitoring your father carefully for further signs of hostility. Your father's family rearranges itself on the lawn—some drawing closer, some shielding their dog-children's eyes from the scene; all of them trying to take it in so they can tell the story later to their friends—until the oldest brother, the chiropodist and acting patriarch, comes mincing toward us from far across the lawn, making reconcil-iatory gestures and softly saying, "Hey-hey-hey-hey, you two, hey-hey," in what he imagines to be a soothing manner.

You are whimpering in my arms.

I kiss you on the mouth.

"Chouette's grandfather tried to drown her in the pool," I say.

"Don't make up more of your stories," your father says. "I saw what happened. You're crazy. You're a danger to yourself and others. You're a danger to your own child. God, I've tried for so long."

The rescue birds don't like his tone. They flap and squawk and screech.

"Now give me our girl, Tiny. Hand her over. No one needs to get hurt."

He tries to take you away from me.

I hear the glorious, true music of Bernard Herrmann's string chorus in my head.

You attack.

Seven

Moments after your father was taken away, owl-baby, your grandmother came running across the lawn with a fireman's axe, and in a fit of mother-passion she chopped up the rescue birds and fed them to the dogs.

I can understand her passion—I have flown into the same kind of a fury on many an occasion when someone tries to harm you, my dear—but your grandmother got it wrong. She blamed the blameless birds. She doesn't blame you at all. None of them do.

I don't blame you, either, Chouette, even though I saw what you did. I witnessed it all. Your ruthless strike was obscured from the rest of your father's family by a flurry of wing and feather, when the gaggle of rescue birds began to have fits just before your father made his grab for you. No one saw what you did except for me. Not even your father knows exactly how it happened. The dirt and grit I had just thrown in his face hid the truth: that you aimed deliberately for your own father's right eye, and then, with utter efficiency, you gouged it out and ate it, while the other birds, innocent martyrs all, merely fluttered and shrieked their approval. Whenever I revisit the memory, I feel an urge to start cheering. Here is my only disappointment: Just after your triumphant act of self-identity—just after you attacked your father and gouged out his eye and ate it—I watched you transform back into a muttish dog-child in my arms, receding from your true self, retreating back into the image of a dog-child that your father wanted you to be, retreating moment by moment from the owl-baby I love and back into the medical experiment that your father made you into. Oh, how I wish I could have kept you here and safe with me! But whatever good the trip to the bottom of the pool did for you disappeared. You stared at the blood on your talons. You looked at the shattered bodies of the birds all around us on the broad lawn. You looked up at your grandmother, whose face was full of rage and grief, and splashed with the blood of martyred birds. You began to cry in big dog-tears. I soothed you the best way I could.

And now your father's family is not quite sure what to think.

It happened so fast. They would like to blame me for all of it. Everything. But how could the mother be to blame, they ask one another, when she was busy taking care of the scream-ing, nearly drowned child in her arms? But then again, what was she doing there, soaking wet and with her weeping child clutched in her arms, making her husband crouch with her amidst the dirt and bird droppings, as if they were a family of wild things? Why would a mother expose her child to that pack of grotesque, mite-infested rescue birds? Could it be that the mother's own hysteria infected the birds, and provoked their aggression, and turned those normally passive creatures into the kind of enraged wild animals that could attack such a gentle and loving man as the husband?

The child's demented grandfather insists that the mother tried to drown her own child.

Who to believe? Which story is true?

Did the mother really try to *drown her own child*?

They are concerned.

They can all agree on that.

We're home again, Chouette. It feels so good to us both to be home again that we rush inside together so we can breathe in the giddy, gamey scent of the place where we belong. But something isn't right. The smell is off. We discover together that while we were away, all the gentle creatures that shared our home, the living things that made up the bulk of your diet, have fled and/or flown or run away—the wood shrews and mice, the rats and spiders—leaving only their nests and their droppings behind. It will take months to restore our habitat to its natural healthy state again. Only the backyard pocket gophers remain.

And here is another cross that we must bear: Your grandmother has come to stay with us. She plans to stay for as long as your father remains in convalescence. I don't know what the woman is trying to prove. She seems to think that without your father around you will be neglected, or in danger. She doesn't trust me. Your grandmother has even hired a "day nurse" to help care for you. You hate this so-called day nurse, and I don't blame you. He wears protective goggles and carries a small stunner at all times.

"We're here to help," my mother-in-law insists, but she keeps her distance.

Even though in the heat of the moment she blamed her rescue birds for the loss of her youngest son's eye, her mother-instinct is nonetheless on the alert. She senses that you pose a threat to her kind. She takes notes all the time, sly malicious notes that she hides under her pillow at night. Notes about the mouse droppings she finds in the linen closet, and the rainbow-molds growing up behind the wallpaper. Notes about the smells that waft and wane throughout our home: smells that strike my mother-in-law as pernicious and uncivilized. Notes about your diet, and its lack of dairy or fresh vegetables. Notes about how you have stopped speaking. I can tell that she and I aren't going to get along from the moment she steps over the threshold and shouts, "Sweet Lord, get the borax!" and rushes back to her car and drives away. She comes back an hour later, loaded up with cleaning supplies—not only borax but also ammonia and bleach, and she is wearing a surgical mask, and her eyes above the mask remind me of her youngest son.

Now that I've discovered how quickly you respond to the *water cure*, I'm determined to give you frequent and aggressive baths until you're yourself again. I soon learn that I can rely on unsupervised snatches of time arriving throughout each day, when you and I are left alone together because your grandmother is napping in a chair, and your day nurse is taking advantage of your grandmother's nap to sneak out the front door for his cigarette break. I use these snatches of time wisely. Little by little I'm getting my girl back again via therapeutic small drownings in the bathtub. Sometimes I can even get you to come into the backyard with me, after your bath, where we have just enough time for you to nab a pocket gopher and swallow it up before your day nurse finishes his third cigarette. You're not completely back to your old self. Not yet. You eat the pocket gophers with disturbingly good manners. You never have a bit of viscera left on your face these days. You used to rip and spray guts. Your new fastidiousness must be an aftereffect from your surgery, but I keep faith that, with the help of my *water cure,* one day you'll recover completely.

I hear through the grapevine that today is the day when my husband is coming back from the hospital. He's been away for nine days, getting his eye socket attended to. The more I think about my husband coming home, the more likely it feels to me that, when he gets here, there is going to be a reckoning between us of some kind. And when I think about that reckoning to come, I feel so many feelings. The feelings grow and keep getting bigger until they're so huge that I can't keep them inside any longer. They don't fit in me. They're tearing me apart. They rip a hole right through my chest, and my heart comes a-tumble out, in the shape of my owl-lover.

"There you are," my owl-lover says simply.

"There you are yourself," I say.

I haven't seen her since the time we argued in Berlin, and here she is again. We don't know what to say. We're afraid to touch or speak. I'd forgotten how enormous she is. Her wing-span must be twelve feet across, and my chest-cavity is none too large. She's feeling cross after being cramped in such a tiny space for so long a journey, without even a window seat to make the trip more bearable.

"I can't stay long," she says.

She's looking at me with those same fond eyes. I'm filled with sharp emotion. Already I'm weeping, weeping, because I want what's happening to be the real thing, and not one of my woolgatherings that I make up now and then to make life more tolerable. My owl-lover snaps me back to reality with a peck on my cheek, and I decide that she is here for real, in all of her dark wonder, filling up my kitchen and knocking the dishes over on the counter and gazing down at me with tender love.

"You need to focus, my love," she says. "We don't have much time. I've come to warn you. Something's up. Our child is in danger."

"I know," I say. "But what do I do?"

I can see all the days and hours that we loved each other reflected in her shallow, fierce crossed-penny eyes. I see when we were children, gathering rainbows from the trees. I see us hunting swallows and starlings in the wildwood groves.

I see me making love with this glory-monster, on the night we made a child of our own. I want to tell her how sorry I am that I wasn't the kind of partner she could count on to be her forever-love. It's all in the past, though, because I've chosen to live this other kind of life, where I'm a little wife, and a little mother, and all of the magic and music has been drained right out of me.

I'm small and weak and helpless.

"Stop thinking you're helpless," she says. "You're not. You're the strongest person I know. Remember that when the time comes. Trust in your love for that kid, and you'll be all right. You're one tough cookie, and so is our girl."

Then my tender-lover makes a sound that I have always loved, low in her throat and peaceful.

I've never seen anyone so beautiful.

She kisses me.

It's a good-bye kiss.

"It's time to tell," she says.

She climbs back into the hole she made in my chest and pulls herself inside, and after she pulls in every feather, she sews me shut again, from the inside, in small, neat stitches.

It's up to me now.

Later that day I'm washing the walls of your nursery, owl-baby, and you're singing one of your eerie incantatory melodies from your crib, and even though I'm expecting him back that day, neither one of us is fully prepared for what happens next, which is that your father, back from the hospital and wearing a jaunty patch over one eye, strides into your nursery as if he thinks he belongs there. He barely says hello to me before he starts in on one of his random soliloquies.

"I should have seen how much help you needed," he says. "I should have seen it long ago."

Yabber-yabber.

I'm having trouble following his string of words because I'm trying to decide what I think of his jaunty eye patch. His patch is leading me to ruminate nostalgically over our experiences as parents of an owl-baby: over all the long years of our twists and turns together, in this lifelong, epic parent-feud of ours. My husband won't stop his yabber-yabber long enough for me to get a word in edgewise, and so I must nod and wink at him to communicate my thoughts. "It's been quite the battle, hasn't it?" my eye-wink says to him. And my husband's eye-wink answers: "You're right, dear wife, it's been quite the battle, and we wear the battle scars to prove it—I, my jaunty eye patch, and you, your fashionable dueling scar."

"My damn work," my husband is saying. "My damn obsession with finding a fix for our girl. I didn't see the signs. My God, how did it come to this. All these years I thought you were looking after our girl when you were doing her harm. It's time for you to get the help you need. You'll like the doctors at this place. They're the best experts. When I think of what you've done to our girl. I hope you can understand what I'm saying, Tiny."

"No," I say. "No, I can't understand you."

"It's for the best," he says. "My mother wanted you charged with criminal negligence. She called the gendarmes. They were on their way. But I told them that you don't belong in jail. God, no. You're sick. You're not a criminal. I've shielded you. I love you."

You've begun to laugh outrageously from your crib, Chouette, mocking your father's pompous speech and making small threatening gestures in the direction of his remaining eye. Your father doesn't notice. He carries on grandiosely.

"You need to go," he says. "You're sick. You have no choice, is what I mean. Look at yourself. Can't you see you need help? Don't you know how hard this is for me? Don't you know how much I care for you?"

And when I don't answer—because I don't want to answer—he shifts to a softer approach and says, "Don't you trust me?" and "Don't you want to get better?" and on and on as he rubs my shoulders and kisses my dirty hair. His warm breath on me feels like a promise. He keeps talking and talking. "There's my Tiny," he says. "There's the smile I love. All right, honey, we're all set. Your bag is packed. It's in the trunk. I can send the rest of your things to you later. Whatever you need. Just go freshen up a bit. Your body odor is acting up again. The engine is running. We're ready to go. I'll keep an eye on Charlotte while you freshen up."

I won't let him take you away from me.

I won't go.

"I won't go," I say.

Your father's face, which only moments ago wore a pleasant,

wistful, loving expression, now wears an expression of stiff-beaten egg whites, and he says to me coldly, "Look, honey, I can't take this any longer."

"I can't take this any longer, either," I say.

I hear birds' wings, flapping faintly, a whisper at the window that tells me help is coming; and then the birds force their way inside—at first just a few birds and then multitudes. Their screams and wing-beats deafen me.

"*Omnes moriemini*," the birds shriek.

It's time to tell.

Sometimes I remember a window where there was no window before, right there in the wall, next to the place where I last saw your father. Sometimes I think there was a harsh interrogative light shining in through the window, showing us the way. Sometimes I remember a veritable bird-army pouring in through the window and coming to our aid, and at other times I remember that it was just you and me on our own, owl-baby, doing what needed to be done.

One thing I'm sure about: Your father is not at his peak strength that day. His muscles have withered from his nine days of languishing in a hospital bed while he was recovering from the sudden loss of one eye. And we have the advantage of surprise. No one knows about the hours and hours that we've spent honing our attack skills in the night. Your father may outweigh me by ninety-seven pounds—or maybe just a bit less, given his recent hospital stay—but look how easily

I separate him from his other eye, zip-and-slash! And now that he's blind, you finish the job with one swift cut across the throat. Your father bleeds out. He's no longer a threat to us. His mother takes even less time. When we're done with her, she's an empty husk. Now it's time to take care of the day nurse. He's a fit young fellow, even if he is a smoker, and he takes more effort, but we still have the element of surprise working in our favor because the first two went without a peep. His little stunner never comes out of its holster.

Your face, Chouette, is as blank and hard as the faces of these three on the floor. You look upset. Your face is streaked with blood. Where is my ruthless girl? Is Doctor Great's box of *synthetic intelligence* still doing its work inside your head, in spite of my best efforts to short it out with my *water cure*? Oh, darling, darling, darling! It's not your fault that you're confused! I snatch you up. It's time to tell. Away we will fly, toward light and hope. Life is, in fact, a battle, and the pursuit of goodness is a fragile aspiration when survival calls for ruthless cruelty, especially from mothers.

After the recent sudden carnage in the household we're both so overcome with bloodlust that it's hard to think straight. But I'm a mother, and for my child's sake I need to push the bloodlust out of my head and return my thoughts to practical matters. It's time for steely-cold thinking about how to save ourselves. If we stay here too long, then the dogs will smell blood and will come for us. There will be no explaining things away this time, Chouette. We must fly away quickly. Never to return. For the last time I gaze upon the face of my former husband as he pools and congeals. I see my mistakes so clearly now. My husband's mouth and eyes have become trapped in a permanent rictus of surprise, and he looks up at me accusingly, as if to say: "If that's how you felt, then why did you stay with me for so long?" His complaint is legitimate. I never belonged in his family, Chouette, and you belonged even less than I. Your father might have been a good provider, but his faults loomed large, and he never understood either one of us, and now I have no choice but to finally do the right thing and to leave him.

Let me tell you what's going to happen next, my darling. I've seen it all unfold before in a dream so deep and true that it must have been a premonition. As soon as we climb out of this little window, we'll see a woman painting daisies on her mailbox. There will be a little dog dancing on her lawn. The dog will show us the way. We'll follow that dog forever and we'll never get tired. We'll leave the blocks and straight-edged streets behind us, and we'll come to a wood, where the trees will grow more gnarled and frequent, and the thicket more tangled, and the sky more rainbow, and at long last we'll come to the edge of all things, where the gleaming meets the gloaming. We'll follow the dog right over to the other side. The trees will bend their branches toward us and make us welcome. We'll feel at home right away. You'll see. We'll come to a small house, and after we knock, your other-mother will open the door, and she will embrace us both in her bright-dazzle wings. "Oh, come on in," she'll say, and all of our years of strife and regret will disappear in an instant. The Bird of the Wood will be there, too, a little older, and a little slower, but as full of love as ever. She'll be knitting socks by the fire, and we'll live as we were meant to live, before I made so many mistakes in life, and before I left my true love for a dog-man who couldn't train me to obey his simplest commands. "I knew you'd come back to me one day," my owl-lover will say; and she will look at you fondly, Chouette, and say: "What a strong, good woman must have raised you, kid! She has raised you up so well!"

Our joy will be complete.

Our story will be done.

But that's not what happens.

Here is what happens.

I carry you in my arms. You don't fight me. After we leave the house, we don't see a little dog or a woman painting daisies on her mailbox. All I see is trash and yellow weeds in the yard. Never mind. Your father's car is in the driveway, and the engine is running, just as your father promised. After all of my years of soft capitulations, they won't be expecting anything like this from me. We'll have a head start. We'll drive in this warmed-up car to the place where the wild and untamed thatches begin. Once there, we'll hide the car and we'll make our way through thicket and stream, until we come to a place where we can hide together forever and be safe.

"Where are we going, Mother?" you say.

It still shocks me each time you speak in dog-words, especially when what you say makes sense in context, but I answer your question the best way I can.

"I'm going to rescue you, Chouette," I say. "I'm taking you away from here. I should have done it long ago, but my faith in myself was too small to think I ever could. But now I'm going to take you away to a place where you can finally be yourself. You'll grow up the way you're meant to grow up. I'm taking you home. I'm taking you now."

"Trip, skip, chirrup, I crush and kill and rip," you say.

I take it that you're agreeing with the plan and so I back out and drive off. We leave the main roads as quick as lickety-split before anyone can spot us. Our way is unpaved and uncertain. We drive for miles along the roads and washboarded byways until I pull the car behind a stand of wild bushkit and cut the engine.

"I'm afraid," you say.

"Don't be afraid," I say. "You need to be strong."

"Why?"

You look at me passively, your wild energies temporarily subdued by current events.

"I'm on your side, Chouette," I say. "I'm your mother and I love you. You need to trust me on this one."

You nod, slowly, the way owls do. Your gesture reminds me so much of your other-mother that it leaves me feeling hopeful and brave.

I unstrap your adaptive car seat.

We scramble up a bank.

Everyone has always thought of me as the weak one, as

the quiet and compliant one, as the one they can tell what to do. No one thinks of me as having talons of my own. No one imagines that I could see the day coming when you would need to be rescued from extinction, Chouette, and that I, your mother, would be the one to rescue you.

No one thinks I know how to wash the blood off of us in this irrigation ditch.

We hide until dark, and then we travel silently across the fields and furrows until we get to the road I'm looking for.

A man driving a big truck full of tomatoes stops for us right away.

He has very few teeth, and he's not afraid of you at all.

"My cousin has a little girl just like your little girl," he says.

The man with very few teeth drops us off in a cow-town, and from there we travel by bus until we get to a dust-town, where we hop a bus that is going to the big-town. You fall asleep in my arms. Your face is peaceful. As I look out the window in the natural course of our long journey, I come to a startling realization: that the world is populated not only by dog-people, but by all kinds of people, by cow-people and wolf-people, armadillo-people and cat-people, toad-people and nomads, and small-town librarians; and I can see them all out there being themselves, with no one in the world to tell them to be someone else instead. They're waiting at bus stops, and peering out car windows, and crossing in cross-walks. They're embracing in optimistic, joyful celebration of their love for one another. They're selling melons and cabbages. They're digging ditches. The wonder of the world outside my window plunges me into a feeling close to religious revelation. I wrestle with the bus window until I crack it open. I inhale and feel a profound and nearly erotic attraction to the scents coming through the window, which are mostly a mix of diesel and sage.

You're awake now. You sit in my lap like a small prophet.

By the time our bus pulls into the big-town, it's almost dawn. We've traveled through a night and a day and another night, but there is something still-not-right about this place, too, and so we board another bus together, the one that I hope will be our last. None of the stops along the route looks exactly right and so we travel on. We must be nearing the end of the line by now. We're the last passengers left. I'm beginning to feel uneasy because there's a cross-gale of a fierce hot wind rising up from the south, and it's blowing so hard that it feels like it's going to roll the bus right over. Dead leaves and dead animals and Dixie cups are flying through the air, and the rain begins to pelt down like bullets, and the brakes on this old bus are screeching like a creature in its death-throes. The bus-man is weaving back and forth while gripping the wheel with ravaged hands. He tries to keep his bus on the road, but it's no use. After the next great gust, we fly off the road and into a tumble-brush thicket and keep on going. Branches flap against the windows. I see tree trunks flash by, and old stones, and rusted bus-carcasses, too, because the land is scarred and scattered with the remnants of times when other bus-men fought and lost the battle to keep their bus on its proper route. We bounce and shake. I hang on to you with all of my strength and hope, Chouette, while my head bangs against hard-iron things. I have thoughts about dying. It seems a likely outcome. We're going to ram into one of the trees for sure, or slam into one of those bus-carcasses.

I'm distracted from my thoughts of dying because an idea has popped into my head that the child in my lap is feeling more substantial and less hollow-boned than she was a moment ago. Yes. There is something strangely unfamiliar about the weight of my child in my lap. There is something different about the space my child is taking up in this world. I've always heard that children grow up overnight, and now I'm thinking maybe this old folk wisdom had it right. I look carefully, and I see the truth: My little girl is growing up before my very eyes. She grows so big that she no longer fits in my lap. She no longer fits in the seat next to me. She no longer fits inside this bus. She's so cramped and unhappy that she pulls the metal roof of this bus back with her beak like it's a sardine can and sticks her head out the top and she keeps growing. She must be three stories high by now. She shrieks with ecstatic joy to feel the wild wind coursing through her tip-feathers. She growls and revels. She is strong. She is monstrously individual. She is sister to the Titans. She is Ozymandias before the fall. She is the bird of omen, dark and foul; she is blood-wed; she is Strix; she is harbinger of war and bringer of death and slaughterer of armies, oh, my Polyphonte!—

She is the girl I raised her to be.

My work is done.

I don't know if I should feel proud or terrified.

Stars and sorrows stream past the open roof, heaven-bound.

The bus-man drives on. He's seen it before.

My girl swivels her great head and looks down at me.

"Are you going to feast upon my liver now?" I say.

"No," my little girl says. "But I'm going to leave you."

And just like that, away she flies, out the torn-open roof of this bus, the way children do.

She's gone.

"Stop this bus!" I shriek.

The bus-man pulls over and looks back at me with half-lidded eyes. As soon as he opens the doors, I rush outside. The bus-man drives on, but I can't worry about that. Where is my child? I look around in a frenzy. The wind shrieks and grabs and the rain tumbles down. All I see are trees, so many trees, a rippling wildwood full of them, crooked-limbed and bent over like old soldiers. I can't find my baby. My baby is lost and alone in this maelstrom. My chest constricts. I begin to run in some direction or another. I feel my toes lengthening and grabbing at the soil like long roots, trying to persuade me to give up and plant myself into the ground, to be a tree. "Oh, no you don't!" I holler, and when I beat at the ground and stamp my feet and don't surrender, the earth gives up on me and I run on.

But where is Chouette? Where are you, my darling?

And then I see her, my big strong girl, as big as a jet plane and flying fast, and flying away, one pulse of wing-beat after the last. Her back is strong. Her soul is fierce. She knows where she's going. When I hear her trill-call flying back over the wind, I still feel a tug at my center—we are still connected, this wild creature and I—and like a dog upon a leash, like an empty wagon behind a team of runaway horses, I'm forced to follow, running through muck and stone and over the rough fallow ground, until the final moment, when the mother-child bond between us finally *snaps* like a thunderclap, and I fall back on the ground, and my child flies free of me.

The rain stops.

The wind dies down until it's no more than an afterthought.

The trees rattle and sigh.

Clouds hang down the color of sour milk.

The sky above me broods and sighs.

You didn't look back. Not once.

What a tiny, stupid life I've led! I gave up everything for you! My husband, my lovers, my years and days and hours, my music, my capacity to love—gave them all away in exchange for toil, blood, and excrement! For you! For nothing! I'm all alone! I rage at that empty place in the sky where you flew off and disappeared until there's nothing left of me but a bitter old woman, one whose rage by now has curdled and warped into a feeling far worse than rage: a hollow feeling, dead-heart, grief-shattered, and bottomless.

You should have eaten my liver.

I've stared so long in the direction where you flew off that the sky over there looks fake, like cheap cloth, like a curtain. If I could reach out my hand and catch a corner of this curtain, then I would pull it away, Chouette, and here you would be, standing here in front of me again. Now that your hiding place has been revealed, you look up at me and cackle, and pretty soon the two of us are laughing in big belly-laughs, to think of how you'd fooled me into thinking you had flown away without me, when all this time you were hiding just a few feet away, behind a curtain; and after we finished laughing, maybe I'd take you by the hand and we'd go to the park.

We'd be the same as ever.

But then, what do you know, a curtain really does open, and a sun springs out from the clouds—slant and orange, the way the sun comes just after a late-afternoon storm has passed—and it warms my bones, and with warmth comes hope, or maybe at least a flicker of hope.

"All right, then!" I shout out recklessly. "Let's see if the world is ready for a creature like Chouette!"

And with these words, I give her up. I let her go. And maybe my heart lightens a little, and maybe not.

All this time the trees around me have been filling up with small anonymous birds. They've been drifting back from their hiding-places, now that the storm has passed. Before long they are singing out in surprise and thanksgiving that they've survived, first with shy cheeps, and then ever more raucously—to be alive after all! to have lived through such a tempest as this!—and their song distracts me from my solitary grief. "*Ave Maria, gratia plena!*" they sing. Maybe I'm persuaded by their chaotic insistence on celebrating their survival. Maybe it's the way they keep reminding me that I'm not the only mother to have lost a child. At any rate, I don't want to die any longer. I'm beginning to wonder, just a little, about what happens next. I begin to imagine making a choice for myself. A choice for me. Only my mind's a blank. I have no idea what I want to happen next.

Even so, I feel the grief resolve in me, at least for now, into something softer, like sadness. I discover, like the birds, that I'm going to make it through this storm. I breathe deep. I look all around. The air smells fresh and everything is rainbow. I hold my head high. And I guess a bus may be back for me, or it may not, but either way I'm beginning to feel like it's my turn.

MUSIC IN *CHOUETTE*

Tiny hears music all of the time, sometimes in her environment and sometimes in her head.

Here is the music that Tiny mentions by name while telling her story:

Arvo Pärt: *Spiegel im Spiegel*
Tom Johnson: *Failing: A Very Difficult Piece for String Bass*
Einojuhani Rautavaara: *Cantus Arcticus*
Wolfgang Amadeus Mozart: String Quartet no. 19 in
   C Major, K. 465
Anna Clyne: *Dance* for cello and orchestra
Robert Schumann: "An meinem Herzen, an meiner Brust"
Antonín Dvořák: *Silent Woods*
Antonín Dvořák: *Miniatures* for two violins and viola
Olivier Messiaen: *Oiseaux Exotiques*
Benjamin Britten: Cello Suite no. 1, op. 72, "Bordone"
Jules Massenet: *Werther*, Act 3, "Va! laisse couler mes larmes!"
Jerome Kern: "Ol' Man River"
Kaija Saariaho: *Sept Papillons* for solo cello

Dimitri Tiomkin: "Gunfight at the O.K. Corral"

Georges Bizet: *Carmen*, Act 4, "Tu m'aimes donc plus"

Henryk Górecki: Symphony no. 3, op. 36, *Symphony of Sorrowful Songs*

Isaac Watts: "My Shepherd Will Supply My Need" (American folk melody)

Pyotr Ilyich Tchaikovsky: Symphony no. 6, *Pathétique*, "Allegro molto vivace"

Johannes Brahms: *Ein Deutsches Requiem*, "Denn alles Fleisch, es ist wie Gras"

Igor Stravinsky: *Rite of Spring*, arranged for two pianos

Bernard Herrmann: *Psycho*, "The Murder"

But Tiny doesn't always recognize the music she hears, especially if it's not from the Western classical tradition. Even if she knows the music, she is sometimes too distracted to mention it by name as she tells her story.

When Tiny first runs away into the gloaming as a child, the music she hears beckoning to her through the trees is "Cambria," by Patricia Taxxon.

When Tiny attends a concert in Berlin, she hears Beethoven's "Leonore no. 3" Overture, op. 72.

When Tiny is pregnant and she visits her mother-in-law's home for the Thanksgiving Feast, the rescue birds sing "Ave Maria, gratia plena" to her, as composed by Hildegard von Bingen.

When Chouette plays her little marimba for the first time, she is playing a passable solo rendition of "Claviers" by Iannis Xenakis, but her mother doesn't recognize it. Like many mothers, even those who think their children can walk on water, Tiny doesn't always fully appreciate or even comprehend her child's unique inner life.

After Chouette flies away for good, the birds that come back from the storm to roost in the trees sing Javier Busto's "Ave Maria gratia plena" to Tiny, to console her.

At the end of her story, when Tiny resolves to be joyful no matter what her future brings, in her head she hears "The Stars in My Head," by Patricia Taxxon.